DARK CELEBRATIONS

Books by Calvin Demmer

Short Story Collections
The Sea Was a Fair Master
Dark Celebrations
The Town That Feared Dusk

DARK CELEBRATIONS

CALVIN DEMMER

TABLE OF CONTENTS

HUNGRY GHOSTS...7

LABOR DAY HUNT 27

TRICK OR DEATH 49

THANKS SINNING..69

THREE DEAD MEN 89

HAPPY DARK YEAR 109

DYING VALENTINE...127

SPRING OUTBREAK 147

SHE WILL RISE 165

PROM SCREAMS 183

UNIDENTIFIED FATHERLY OBJECT.......................201

INDEPENDENCE DENIED 223

Bonus story
LEPRECHAUN LUCK...243

HUNGRY GHOSTS

TEN TIPS FOR SURVIVING THE HUNGRY GHOST FESTIVAL
1. Do not interfere with any offerings. If done by accident, immediately apologize aloud.
2. Do not open an umbrella indoors, as it may invite ghosts.
3. Do not marry, start a new business, or move home during ghost month.
4. Do not wander after midnight.
5. Chopsticks placed upright are a direct invitation for ghosts to partake in your meal.
6. Do not sleep facing a mirror or reflective surface. This may guide ghosts to you.
7. Do not pat anyone's shoulder or forehead. It brings them bad luck and puts them at risk of being possessed.
8. Do not swim. Drowned evil ghosts seek victims for their rebirth.
9. Do not take photos, selfies, or videos. Ghosts may appear.
10. Do not turn around if a voice calls you from behind.

* * *

Dusk had drawn closed like a curtain all round Lara Adams. Straining her eyes, she tried to read the squiggly red font on the small cream-colored card in her hands. She was thankful it was in English and not Chinese. The air was getting cooler, and the warmth of energy she felt earlier in town departed. On her sides, rows of mature trees stood tall. The stone path under her feet had lost its white-and-blue color. It knew only gray tones now.

Shaking the agitation growing within her, she held the card closer to her eyes. A receptionist from the hotel had given it to her. The woman had insisted she take one, even when Lara tried to wave her off. The title on the card read: *TEN TIPS FOR SURVIVING THE HUNGRY GHOST FESTIVAL*, but it was the first line that held Lara's attention.

She turned to her boyfriend, Ray Jimenez. "You see, here it says you shouldn't disturb the offerings they set out for the ghosts. That's why the old guy alongside the road fumed with anger when you knocked over the bowl of food. It was for the ghosts. You should've just apologized."

There was no reply. Ray had stopped in the middle of the path. His head swung from left to right and back again. He rested his hands on his hips.

"Ray? Did you hear me?" Lara asked, moving strands of her curly brunette hair away from her eyes. She was still adjusting to her new haircut. Her hairdresser back home had guaranteed it was in style, that it suited her round face and showed off her beautiful emerald-green eyes.

Ray placed his index finger over his lips.

The agitation boiled to anger within Lara. Friends often teased Ray that he looked like a lost Jonas brother with his pitch-black hair and boy-next-door looks. He was anything but cute or handsome to her now.

She couldn't help but think back to how their relationship began. Ray had been a second-string receiver at college, though you wouldn't have thought so with his slight frame, but he was fast and had great athletic ability. Lara had been on the volleyball team, perfect for her tall, slender body. The two met during a party held for the various sports teams. She once yearned for his attention, but now, because she desired more in a relationship, she had her doubts about anything more serious evolving between them. It seemed as if the time they had spent dating in college and the few months together out of it would be the full timeline of their relationship. Even the holiday was failing to spark any new life into the relationship. If anything, it was only showing how different the two of them were.

They vacationed in China, her first time abroad. The trip had started well, especially when they realized they'd arrived during the Hungry Ghost Festival, or *Zhong Yuan Jie*, as the locals called it. City markets and squares were abuzz during the afternoon, with people lighting candles, playing traditional music, and leaving food out for the ghosts. Lara and Ray had watched a young girl singing on stage in the afternoon. Before the stage were a few rows of empty seats cordoned off from the public. Apparently, they reserved seats for any ghosts who wanted to catch the performance. As it grew later, people lit incense all around, while leaving papier-mâché clothing and gifts in various spots for the ghosts. At first, Lara had found the festival a little creepy, but as she noticed the joy and warm vibe of all the people, she took pleasure in it as well.

"Ray, are you ignoring me?"

Ray wasn't answering. He was back to looking around, scratching the side of his face.

"Wait, don't tell me. You don't know where we're going, and you're getting us lost?"

Ray turned to her. "Chill, Lara. I'm only scoping the place out. Care to have a little faith in me?"

Soft crackling sounds alerted Lara to something at her side. She whipped her head toward the noise and stared at one of the bushes at the foot of the crooked tree near her. The spicy, earthy aroma overwhelmed her senses, but she knew it was because her adrenaline was kicking in. She hoped it wasn't some type of wild animal. Lara wasn't sure which, if any, animals inhabited the area. This only allowed her imagination to grow with the possibilities of what strange creature it could be. This was never a good thing.

She clapped her hands, but the noise didn't abate. It became louder. Lara feared she had provoked the animal.

It headed straight for her.

* * *

Once, when Lara had been a young girl hiking with her father, she'd experienced a similar episode. They had been on a dirt path alongside a line of tall pine trees and low-growing plant life when rustling bushes alerted her to something approaching, something she couldn't see. She tensed up and stopped walking. When her father placed his hand on her shoulder, the fear dissipated. "What's wrong, honey?" he asked. Lara told him about the sound coming from the bush. "Oh, it's probably just a squirrel," her father replied. He turned out to be right. The little critter darted out from its hiding place and ran across the path ahead of them.

Ray placed his hand on her shoulder, as her father had done, except the fear didn't leave. Nor did the creature in the bush reveal itself.

"What's wrong? You look like you've seen a ghost," Ray said.

The concern was still circulating in Lara's limbs. She considered bolting up the path until she found civilization, but she didn't. She was an adult now. Her father wouldn't always be around to provide a guiding hand, and she didn't want to rely on Ray. She ignored the frigid weight that such a thought brought and focused on controlling her emotions.

"Come out, little critter," Lara said to the bush as she kneeled.

Ray looked at her as if she had lost her mind, but she ignored him. He'd gotten them lost because he wanted to go for a stroll, and she knew the walk was because he had other desires. Ray would be getting no action tonight.

"Come here, little one. Don't be afraid," she said.

"Lara, it's too scared. Whatever it is you think is in the bush, it isn't going to come out now."

Lara ignored Ray. She remained still, waiting for the creature to appear from its hiding spot, hoping to prove a point to Ray. Darkness was coming quick, and she didn't like the idea of being away from the reassuring lights of town, especially in a foreign country. Tapping her foot, she counted down from a hundred in her mind. She could hear Ray mumbling beneath his breath as he walked behind her.

Ray went quiet, and so too did the world.

Two hands gripped her from behind. A guttural roar followed. Lara screamed, turning around. Instinctively, she swung her hands at whatever had grabbed her. Ray dodged her swings while releasing her. He laughed. The sound echoed in the night air.

"Ha-ha, gotcha," he said. "You just shit yourself."

"You're such an asshole." Lara stepped away from Ray. "You probably scared the thing off now."

"I scared you. That's for sure." Ray held his hand up for a high five as he walked to her.

Lara turned away from him, her gaze back on the bush that had first caught her attention. Ray was still chuckling, but he knew better than to touch and console her now.

"All right, all right. Come on, Lara. Let's get going, then."

Lara didn't reply. Him frightening her only compounded the agitation that had been building up within her. Creeping near the bush, she leaned forward. Lara wasn't sure if she was really looking for the animal, or if she was just making Ray wait a while. She didn't care either way.

"Here, little one," she said, knowing it would annoy Ray.

She was right. Ray cursed and kicked at the path. Lara decided to wait and see if his demeanor changed. Maybe he'd even apologize after his little fit. Keeping one eye on the bush that had gone still, an uneasy feeling tugged in her core. It was disappointing how the trip was souring. Ray's language become viler as he cussed his own luck for having a girlfriend as mature as a twelve-year-old. There would be no apology, but later there would be an argument.

Getting bored of punishing Ray, Lara drew her focus back to the fact that Ray didn't know where he was leading them. He had already edged forward along the path after seeing her crouch down by the bush. She stood and crossed her arms.

"I'm done," she said.

Ray kept walking. Lara wasn't sure if he was pretending not to hear her, so she raised her voice. "Ray, did you hear me? I'm done."

He turned around, shaking his head. "Done with what? Please tell me we aren't going to have another scene?"

"I'm done with . . . with this evening stroll. I think it's best if we turn around and go back."

The crackling sound returned. Something was alongside them, but it moved away from Lara now. She could tell by the speed with which it travelled that it had no intention of going back into hiding. She looked up the path toward Ray. A dark shape, about half his length, came out from the safety of the bushes. Ray held his arms out to defend himself. Lara moved forward and to the side, only to see that it wasn't a critter at all. A young boy with pitch-black hair in a gray shirt was standing ahead of Ray. The boy was panting as he held his hands up like an officer directing traffic.

"Holy shit," Ray said. "You scared the crap outta me, dude."

"No go back," the boy said. "No go back. I show you shortcut to town."

Ray looked toward Lara, who knew he was seeking her approval after annoying her when he had frightened her. She focused on the boy. "Have you been following us? We heard a sound in the bushes."

The boy shook his head.

Lara considered her options. She wasn't sure if the boy was lying or not, and she was curious why the boy didn't want them to go back the way they had come. She figured he likely wanted a reward if he got them back to town quicker.

"That sounds great, thank you." Lara approached Ray and the boy. "What's your name?"

"Gen."

"Well, Gen, if you get us back quick, Ray over here will give you a nice reward. Does that sound good?"

Gen nodded and smiled. Ray frowned.

"Lead the way," Lara said.

Gen wasted no time as he turned on the spot and paced into the darkness ahead of them. Lara set off after him, passing Ray. He called after her, but she didn't respond.

Catching up with the boy, Lara decided to walk alongside him. She may not have known her surroundings well, but she sensed they were going in an odd direction to find the town they came from. In fact, it seemed as if they were moving farther away. She decided to trust the boy, figuring the path may have had a slight curve and would soon lead back into another part of town. The landscape around her was fast becoming wilder while the sounds of insects were getting louder. Away from the lights of town, the night seemed blacker than she had experienced before, even darker than on any of the camping trips she'd gone on with her family. If not for the starry sky above, Lara realized that she and Ray would have gotten lost for sure. She had seen other routes escaping from the main one they were on during their stroll. It would have been easy to take a wrong turn.

Thankfully, Gen had found them.

* * *

It didn't take long for Ray to pass Lara and make his way alongside Gen. He chatted and then joked with the boy. Lara had moved back, walking a few feet behind the two of them. She listened and couldn't help but smile every now and again. Once, she almost laughed aloud, but she quickly slapped her hand over her mouth before the sound could escape. This was her problem with Ray. He had so many endearing qualities, like how good he was with kids, but it was his other immature hang-ups that'd worn her through. Would trying to sit down and have a serious conversation with him help? A part of her still wanted Ray to grow up and become the man she believed he could be. Shaking her head, she cursed her own indecision. That was the problem with emotions. They sat on a fine line, always threatening to tip the scale one way or another. It's why her father always told her never to make a major decision on an impulse.

A bite in the air pulled Lara from her thoughts. They had been walking a while, and yet she still didn't see the bright activity of town. Focusing ahead, she realized she wasn't quite correct. There were lights, but they were a warm orange, and they shifted when directed by a breeze. Nearing, she saw little candle lanterns attached all along a bridge ahead of them. She heard the gentle sound of running water. An ashy aroma hung in the air.

The narrow wooden bridge, crossing a small river, was barely above the water. On its sides were thin dark wooden beams that supported the curved handrail. The river flowed calmer than she first assumed, and it shimmered under the spell of the sky above. The atmosphere had become peaceful, and apart from the river, no noise traveled through the space around them. The place was scenic, soothing. The earlier tension of being away from town eased within Lara, though it didn't vacate her completely.

"This is beautiful," Ray said. "You have to admit that."

"Yeah, it is," Lara said. "But we have to get a move on."

"Hang on. Just give me a second, jeez."

Lara shook her head. Gen seemed indifferent to their squabble, though he did turn his head to admire the bridge once or twice.

"Wow." Ray made his way to the right side of the bridge. "Have a look over here. There's a light in the water. I wonder if they put something in it for the festival."

Lara sighed but went to him.

A strange illumination emanated from within the river. It didn't look like any decoration she could recall, and it was too bright to be a reflection from the sky above. Lara crooked her neck, trying to see what could be making the light. Slowly, something seemed to be coming up from beneath the surface. Ray had also grown more curious and crouched down onto his knees, pushing his head between two beams of the wooden railing.

A pale white hand broke the surface. Lara gasped as the fingers curled like claws. She blinked, trying to refresh her view, hoping it would be gone. Gen was a little bit farther on the bridge now, and he seemed to smile with the appearance of the unexpected extremity. The hand moved in Ray's direction, and he attempted to knock it away, but it got hold of his wrist. Lara screamed but was too late. It tugged Ray's arm with what Lara could only think of as an incredible force, because it yanked him into the river. His body broke through two of the wooden rails as he left the bridge. The splash sent water shooting into the air. Some cool droplets landed on Lara's face.

"Oh my God," Lara said, holding her hands out. "What the hell is that? Ray? Ray, where are you?"

She crouched, only to feel two small hands press on her back. Turning around, Lara found Gen trying to push her into the river, but he wasn't strong enough. She held onto a beam of the railing, and she pushed back at Gen, sending him falling back onto his rear.

Returning her view to the river, Lara only saw darkness, and a dirty cloud forming where Ray had fallen in. Keeping herself locked in place with her shoulder against the beam, fearful Gen may try to push her again, she leaned forward. There was still no sign of Ray, but she identified the strange black cloud.

Blood.

A hand stretched out from the cloud. It tried holding onto the side of the bridge. Lara was ready to kick out, but she stopped when Ray's head broke the surface. She tried to grab his hand, but he pulled it away.

"Run, Lara. For God's sake, run," Ray said, half gurgling. His head and hand returned below the surface.

Lara moved back. Ray's head broke the surface again. This time there was something on his shoulders. Tangled black streaks curled around his neck. They shifted, and Lara saw the face that had hid beneath the mop of long black hair. It chilled her to the core. She couldn't decide if it resembled a corpse, or zombie, or something worse, but whatever it was, it didn't belong in this realm. The pale thin abomination put its claw-like hand under Ray's throat and dug its long yellow nails into his throat. Blood spurted all over the side of the bridge.

"Oh my God, Ray!" Lara jumped up, watching in horror as the creature pulled Ray back into the watery realm.

Gen grabbed her by the arm. "No, you can't go. My sister must feed, feed until full. Please, we have tried *ti shen*, but drowning people doesn't work for her. Like some of the other ghosts have discovered, we have found that eating people allows her to continue in her own body for a while longer."

Lara slapped him across the face, which sent him reeling backward. Tears built in his eyes, and he stood, staring her down. A sinister darkness took over his visage, a darkness she hadn't seen on the innocent boy earlier. She didn't know what was in the river; Gen had called it a ghost. If it was, it didn't resemble the nearly see-through spirits she recalled seeing floating around on films and documentaries.

A fact did slap Lara awake, however. There was nothing she could do for Ray. The ghost in the river was too powerful. The only choice she had was to escape. Maybe she could get help, maybe it would be too late, and maybe she wouldn't even get away. Her heart thundered as all the conflicting emotions swelled within her. Like a strike of lightning illuminating a nighttime sky, her next action was clear.

Lara ran.

She ran through questions in her mind. She ran over other feelings that wanted to rise within. Lara ignored Gen's screams as he called for her to return. Darting on the path, she headed back the way they had originally come from. Fearful that Gen or the ghost of the river may know her route, she decided to duck into the trees.

She tried to keep her bearings as her pace slowed. Only when she thought she heard a voice close behind did her speed increase over the difficult terrain.

Something snatched her right foot; the ground rushed toward her face.

* * *

Lara opened her eyes, and the dusty soil filled her view. There was no monster. She had tripped on the creeping roots of a tree. The river, which had grown stronger, was still audible. Fortunately, she'd made it deep enough into the realm of trees that Gen and the ghost hadn't found her, but she knew the horrific event had been true. Fragmented images of the ghost of the river attacking Ray bounced in the fore of her mind. There had been so much blood. She heaved but quickly got her hand over her mouth to stop herself from retching.

Lara couldn't make any noise.

She wasn't safe.

Feeling around her head for any cuts or bumps, she got to her knees. She shifted forward as she touched the large bruise on the side of her forehead. The bruise beat upon discovery, but Lara braced through the pulsations. The path was near. She reminded herself to breath as she prepared to survey the area around the river.

Lara could see them in the distance. She didn't want to believe it, but her mind refused to betray her. They had followed her. Gen held something in his hand. It looked like an arm. Lara gagged, realizing the limb could belong to Ray.

"*Chī, chī, chī,*" Gen said.

It was one of the few Chinese words Lara knew. Gen was saying, "Eat, eat, eat."

The ghost, whom Gen had called his sister, looked less pale and gaunt than earlier; at least that's what Lara sensed at first. The spectral sister raised her arm as if reaching for Ray's limb. She didn't grab it. Instead, she turned and pointed at the bushes, straight at Lara.

"Oh shit," Lara said, getting to her feet.

Lara didn't wait, and burst out of the bushes, running in the direction of the town; at least she hoped she had guessed the right way. Disorientation still hampered her mind after her fall. She ignored Gen's call from behind, and then she ignored the patter of little feet coming after her.

With her chest burning as she ran, Lara yearned for the lights of civilization. The area did look familiar, but she couldn't be sure she wasn't fooling herself. A pain, like a steel rod impaling her heart, exploded in her chest as she thought of Ray. She tried to pick her speed up, hoping the increased burning would force her to focus on her escape.

Candles appeared on the path, surely a good sign because she remembered those from when they had first left the safety of town. Except most of them were out or knocked over. There were broken bowls and food lying farther up, as well as ripped-up papier-mâché clothing, and other destroyed gifts. If this was the work of ghosts like the one of the river, it was clear they were after more than the offerings.

Lara swallowed hard. She hoped it was merely the work of kids or drunkards.

Something gray, like an ashen branch, shot out of a bush near her. Lara was slow to move out of its way, realizing too late that it was an arm. The hand grabbed her ankle.

Lara fell forward, using her arms to shield her face from crashing onto the stone path. She knew if she passed out this time from a fall, she would never wake up. The action worked even though the pain that shot through her limbs felt like knives slashing at her forearms. She pushed up. Her attacker crawled to her. It was a man, except it wasn't a normal man. It was a decayed ghost, like the one from the river. This ghost had no legs, however, and Lara moved back, trying to ignore the fatigue and aches.

"Get away, get away," Lara said, lifting her leg higher. She was ready to kick the creature in the head if it didn't obey.

The ghost opened its mouth. A gurgling sound came out as its bottom jaw dropped lower than what should be possible. Blood dripped from its purple lips. The few rotten teeth it had left were ready to bite.

Lara kicked it.

Her foot landed against the upper right side of the ghost's face. A *pop* preceded its right eye dropping to the ground. It seemed undeterred by the loss of the body part.

Lara got to her feet, dodged a desperate lunge from her attacker, and turned to run.

Movement came from the sides of the path. More of the ghosts were coming; she tried not to look as she bolted past. Her lungs didn't burn as badly as they did after escaping Gen and his unnatural sister, because a new spike of adrenaline gave her the boost she needed.

There were lights in the distance.

* * *

The town's main street was near empty when Lara burst into it. Gone were the crowds of people and stalls from earlier that day. There were still a few candles burning, while a few plates and bowls waited for their intended guests on the sidewalk. Packs of papier-mâché clothing and other gifts had also been untouched. This was a reassuring contrast to the destruction she'd seen outside of town. The air smelled like spices and incense; it was almost pleasant. Lara sought the first open business, but it appeared as if all of them had closed early.

Just ahead, a figure moved in the shadows on the side of the road. Lara stopped. Fragments of light coming from one of the stores illuminated the figure. She didn't know the man, but she recognized his uniform.

"Officer, Officer, please. I need your help," she said, hurtling toward him.

The officer turned around. His deep black hair shone purple at the sides when graced by the light. He was short but looked fit. There were no signs in his movement that he expected anything particularly troublesome this night. He crooked his neck to see Lara better in the dark.

He strolled to her.

"Please, Officer, it got my boyfriend. Oh, my God, it got him." Lara's body shook violently as icy tears ran down her warm cheeks. She worried she would collapse. Now that she was safe, she wanted to give in to her tired body. Maybe if she passed out, the pain from seeing Ray attacked would subside, if even just for a while.

"Where is your boyfriend? Who got him?" the officer asked, reaching for the radio at his side.

"The ghost. It was a ghost in the river. I swear, there was this boy—"

"Wait," the officer said, lifting his hand away from his radio. "This is not funny. You should respect our customs and not make jokes about them. Go now, get to where you are staying, and make no more jokes."

"No, no, no. It was real."

The officer frowned and waved his hand at her as if he were shooing a mosquito from his face. He turned around and walked away.

"Wait, wait," Lara pleaded.

The officer ignored her.

Lara, Lara, Lara.

Lara heard the voice calling from behind. The sound was mellifluous, as if the person was almost singing her name. She sensed her body turning. *Must. Not. Turn.* She didn't want to see what terror was still after her. The encroaching fear pierced her like an icicle to the heart. Maybe the ghost of the river wouldn't let her escape. Even with the dangers thundering in her mind, Lara couldn't resist.

She turned around.

It was Gen's ghostly sister, except she no longer looked like some decomposing bag of flesh and bone. She appeared beautiful, clean, and young. Her long black hair cascaded down her shoulders, touching the nearly see-through white dress she wore. No longer was she pale or gaunt. Her skin had a vibrant tone, and her body a healthy shape. She moved with her back against one of the walls as if she were a leaf guided by a zephyr. She entered a dark shadowy section. Lara waited for her to reemerge.

She didn't.

Lara turned around. The officer was nearly out of sight. Feeling her heart pump within her chest with so much force she feared it would break out of her rib cage, she ran. She moved faster than she ever had, even faster than when she'd bolted from the river. Lara passed the officer, who shouted something at her, but she didn't listen.

All she cared about now was getting out of this place, getting home. The scenes she had witnessed would leave scars in her mind. She didn't doubt she'd have to explain Ray's disappearance, or that she may get into trouble for it once back home. The pain of losing him would never leave. Her first trip abroad had brought her first true nightmare, but all those concerns were secondary thoughts as her brain and heart agreed on their commands. They shouted, "Run, Lara. For God's sake, run."

Lara obeyed.

The ghosts in China were still hungry.

Lara didn't want to be their next meal.

LABOR DAY HUNT

Jared Rodgers felt underdressed and untidy. He wore a wrinkled black shirt and faded denims. Attempts to neaten his curly brown hair had failed. The well-built man shaking Jared's hand wore a pinstripe suit with a black bow tie. His black hair stayed perfectly parted to the side. While everyone was out celebrating Labor Day, Jared was trying to make some extra cash. Two hundred dollars for two hours' work, according to the ad he had seen.

Fresh out of college, he had postponed his dream of exploring the world when his uncle passed away due to a heart attack. Jared couldn't leave his aunt alone to fend against the wolves at the door. He was only twelve when his aunt and uncle had adopted him after his parents both died in a car crash. Instead of leaving Silverfields, another small town of forgotten America, Jared took over running his uncle's electronics store. He had been positive at first, thinking he could turn the store's fortune around. Nothing he tried could halt the fall into the red. New merchandise orders ate any profit the store generated. His uncle had been slow to embrace change, hanging on to electronic relics of the past. This had been the catalyst for the store's steady decline. It was only a matter of time before Jared would have to give his aunt the bad news that the store could no longer operate. He was trying to put some cash together to soften the blow.

Two hundred dollars would help.

"I'm Tim Lewis," the man said, releasing his hand. "Sorry about not greeting you outside, but time's running short."

Jared's hand stung from the man's grip, but he resisted the urge to rub it, not wanting to show any sign of discomfort. "So what exactly are we doing here? The ad wasn't specific, and when I called, you just said to meet you here."

"Ah." Tim smiled. "It's easy work, friend. Easiest money you'll ever make. We're going to serve some people a meal. Nothing to it, really, and I sure do appreciate you helping me out."

Jared frowned. They were in a large abandoned warehouse. He knew the front of the building. A friend of his, Lee Peralta, had spray-painted a flaming skull on the boarded-up, roll-down door that barred anyone entry. They had come in through the back today. Jared hadn't even realized there was a back entrance until Tim pushed a large dumpster away, revealing two green steel doors. The place, however, was a mess. Dirt, grime, and the stench of a dead rat or two ruled the large, open warehouse floor.

Tim led him to the center of the warehouse, where they stopped before an old elevator. Tim assured him that even though the elevator had a few buttons, there was only one floor below. They descended, and a small room as dirty as the one above greeted them. At least there was light, which came as another surprise to Jared.

"Who would eat here?" Jared asked, noticing the two large black sports bags on a rickety wooden table to his left.

Tim walked over to the bags. He opened one and took out a large lock and chain. "A society. They go by the name 'Silverfields Nightlight Society.'"

Jared stepped to his left, trying to peer into the open bag. It was no use; Tim had closed it again. Tim made his way to the elevator. There, he proceeded to run the chain around the bars on the elevator doors. He attached the lock and clicked it shut. A frigid chill crawled down Jared's back.

"How will the society get in? And what kind of society meets in such a shithole?"

Tim smiled. "They're already here. Anyway, I guess you have a right to know the rest. Locking the elevator is part of protocol; they wouldn't want any vagrants or other uninvited guests ruining their get-together. As for them, well, they're just a bunch of old people who meet at the end of summer every year. You know some consider Labor Day to be the end of summer? Well, anyway, I guess they've been doing it since the town's establishment. There aren't many members left, though."

"Are you a member?"

"Fuck no."

"Well, why here?" Jared asked, trying to keep his tingling nerves beneath the surface. A society meeting in a subterranean room in an abandoned warehouse didn't sound like a group he wanted to encounter.

"I think one of them owns the building now, and the place is away from the center of town. Nothing sinister. Don't stress. There's nothing to worry about, nothing at all. We serve them their meal. Then we'll be done."

"What's their meal? Is it prepared? I can't cook."

Tim looked away. "You ask too many questions. Just chill, Jared."

"Yeah, man. Okay, okay."

"Let's go meet them," Tim said, grabbing the two bags on the table. "What do you say?"

* * *

Jared followed Tim down a narrow passageway illuminated only by the light from the room they exited. The smell of ammonia hung in the air while a chill infused the atmosphere. There had been an attempt to clean this section of the warehouse. It wasn't only the smell, but also the dust didn't grind beneath Jared's shoes as it had in the first room. Jared racked his brain, trying to remember the groups and societies in town—Silverfields wasn't big, after all—but nothing came to the fore. Light formed a rectangular box on the wall up ahead to his right. Looking to his left, he paused, inspecting the open doorway. Tim didn't miss a beat and headed straight ahead.

Jared crossed the threshold into the room with trepidation. Tim smiled, making his way to the end of the table. The people were all seated, and they were indeed old, very old. Wrinkled skin, balding hair, and slow movements seemed the norm. Jared couldn't deny he felt the apprehension calm within. Sure, it was still a strange meeting place, but other than to reminisce about the good old days, he could think of no reasons for a bunch of senior citizens to meet. The area itself was sparse. A few ancient pictures of the town clung to the walls, and candles helped the ailing yellow lightbulb hanging from the ceiling. A glass cabinet stood on the far side, housing glasses, plates, and cutlery. The long, narrow wooden table in the center of the room was clearly the main attraction. A hint of the ammonia smell lived in the air, but it wasn't as harsh as it had been in the passageway.

"Hello, everyone," Tim said. "This is Jared. He will be assisting this evening."

"Hello," Jared said.

One or two of the elderly people nodded, but the rest seemed content to ignore his existence. White bowls, sitting in front of the seven members of the Silverfields Nightlight Society, held their attention. There was a thick red substance in the bowls, reminding Jared of homemade tomato soup.

A balding man with gray tufts of hair above his ears sat at the head of the far end of the table. He took his spoon to the bowl before him, tapping the side. The man then took a mouthful of the soup.

He sighed. "Animal? Tim. How disappointing."

"I'm sorry, Alexander," Tim said. "Some things are rather difficult to procure these days."

"Yes, yes, of course. At least the main meal will be enjoyable."

Tim smiled.

"You all right, Tim?" Alexander asked. "You seem different. I'd say a little apprehensive."

"I'm fine, just been a long day." Tim made his way back to Jared. He opened one of the black sports bags on the floor. Obscuring his face as he rummaged inside, he said, "Shall we get started?"

"Yes, yes, please do," Alexander said. "Everyone here is hungry. Slumber is never a pleasant thing to awaken from."

Tim stood and turned to face the table. Jared did a double take. Tim was wearing a gas mask. In one hand, he gripped an automatic rifle, and in the other he held an object that looked like a grenade.

"In the bag, Jared," Tim said. "Grab a gas mask and a gun. Let's get rid of these motherfuckers once and for all."

"Huh?"

Tim turned back to the elderly people seated around the table. He pulled the pin and tossed the grenade. There was almost no delay as a high-pressured *pop* announced the explosive's discharge. A hissing sound followed.

Jared stepped back. His eyes widened as he tried to understand what was happening. He held his hands up instinctively, covering his face. It wasn't flames that engulfed his world when the grenade went off; instead, a green gas swallowed the room. The stench of garlic overwhelmed him. Jared's eyes watered from the burn, and the potent smell singed his nostrils. He bent down and got the mask on.

After a few breaths, the stench was manageable.

Jared scanned the scene, and his brain rocked within his skull. Pale beings with near-featureless faces except for the beady black eyes that flared with anger had replaced the elderly people. Their hands curled into talons; they clawed at the air around them. As if someone had tossed a live Taser in his direction, Jared needed to react. He reached back into the bag near him and grabbed the assault rifle inside on instinct.

"You have failed us, Tim," the thing that had once been Alexander screamed. He, along with the other society members, huddled at the back of the room. The gas had a definite harmful effect on them.

"Fuck you and all your kind. Tonight, you end. I'm sick of being your puppet." Tim raised his rifle.

"You'll pay. You'll both pay," Alexander said.

"What the fuck is going on? What are they?" Jared asked.

"You haven't figured it out? They're vampires. We have to kill 'em all. The garlic gas will only slow them for a bit."

"But—"

Tim fired.

Oddly, the sound of bullets spitting from Tim's gun reminded Jared of the sound popcorn makes when exploding in a pot. His ears rang painfully. There was no relief from the noise in the confined space.

He tightened his grip around the gun.

Two of the vampires on the far side of the room fell as bullets ripped them apart. The rest split up in a panicked frenzy, searching for an escape. It didn't take them long to realize there was only one way out of the room. They headed for Tim and Jared, since the two of them were standing in front of the only exit.

"Safety's off, Jared. Just fucking aim and fire," Tim shouted.

The fright rocked Jared's body into action, and he took a defensive stance. One of the vampires, what may have been a short old lady once, was heading for him with yellow canine-like teeth exposed. Jared pulled the trigger. The gun shook his arms like a mechanical bull tossing a novice rider around. Bullets seemed to fly everywhere but in her direction. She crashed into him, sending him flying into the corner of the room. Jared ignored the bang his head took against the wall. He got to his knees, picking up the rifle.

The vampire was gone, and along with it the others. Silence had fallen over the room, though his ears still rang. The green shimmer from the gas was beginning to dissipate, but the stench of garlic still reigned in the room. He swallowed hard.

Tim said, "Get up, Jared. Get up. Some of them got away. We gotta go and find them."

"What the fuck? What the fuck?"

"There's no time for you to have a panic attack. Get up and help me over here."

Tim moved to the far side of the room, where the two vampires fell. He no longer wore his mask, and he had slung his rifle around his shoulder. In his right hand, he held a sharpened wooden stick.

"The bullets have all been blessed but will only take them down for a while. We must be sure they're dead." Tim drove the wooden stake into the heart of one of the vampires. When he yanked it back out, black gunk splattered on the wall behind him.

"Holy shit," Jared said. "This can't be happening right now. This is not fucking real."

"Oh, it's happening. And we must finish it. They know both of us. Either we hunt them down, or they will come for us."

"You're insane."

Tim shook his head. "It's us or them. Wake up, Jared. Don't you understand? We must get them before they get us."

"But how? They've escaped."

Tim shook his head. "No, Jared. I have the only set of keys for the lock on the elevator. There is no other way out. It's the same trap they used on their victims here for many years. That would have been you, if I hadn't grown sick and tired of being their little slave. I'm not proud of myself for helping them as my father did before me. But it's over now, one way or another."

"I, I—"

Tim drove the stake into the heart of the second vampire. Jared heard a mushy sound, like someone stepping in mud, as the wooden object found the heart.

"All right." Tim attached the gunk-coated stake onto his belt. "Let's find the rest of these bastards."

"This is nuts," Jared said, shaking his head.

* * *

The two men journeyed again down the passageway. This time they headed deeper into the subterranean level of the warehouse. Jared's mind drifted between confinement in some type of surreal dream and a more piercing reality. Why did he answer the ad? He should have known the pay was too good to be true. Here he was, with some man he had never met before today, hunting vampires. He'd seen the old people transform when the garlic gas exploded in the room. There could be no denial. He had to accept what was. Maybe later he could convince himself that this had been some psychotic break. Maybe he could convince himself he passed out in the warehouse and imagined it all. For now, he could sense the danger if he didn't act. He needed to help kill these abominations, these creatures of the dark, the vampires that roamed his hometown. If what Tim said was true, they had planned to hunt him, kill him, and then drink his blood.

Jared had no previous experience with a weapon, but as he'd found out in the room, all it took with an automatic rifle was to aim and fire. He would now expect for the gun to dance in his hands when he pulled the trigger. He didn't like the idea of taking a stake to the vampires' hearts, but if that's what it took to get out of this hell, that's what he would do. He didn't trust Tim, but the man seemed experienced with a gun and had no reservations about using the stake.

Jared would help him take care of the vampires and flee as soon as he got an opportunity.

"We're going to come to two separate large rooms. You go left, and I'll go right," Tim said, stopping.

"What? You mean split up?"

"Yes." Tim scratched around in the sports bag. He took out some strange-looking black goggles and placed them on his face. He chucked a pair at Jared.

"What's this for?"

"Night-vision goggles. Put them on. I'm not sure if any of the lights work up ahead. If you see one of them, fire. Do not hesitate." Tim reached back into the bag and passed a stake to Jared. "Then stab them in the heart with this. Do you understand?"

"Yeah."

Tim didn't wait for any small talk and marched down the passageway. Jared tried to keep up as he put the goggles on. He almost crashed into the wall on his left because the new equipment seemed to impair his vision more than improve it, and he didn't enjoy the fact that his view was narrower than he liked. Any shadow, any opening, could be hiding one of the vampires. Tim turned sharply to the right and disappeared from view. Jared looked to the arching entrance of the dark warehouse room on his left. Inhaling deeply, he summoned what courage he could find within, scraping bare any reserves.

He turned into the room, bumping his shoulder as he did.

Trying not to curse, he kept focused.

Wearing the goggles forced him to swivel his head to try and get a decent view in the dark area, and he failed to get a proper grasp on his surroundings. Panic threatened to set in. He removed the goggles and ran his hands over the wall nearest to him. A deep crack in the wall caused him to flinch, but after cursing beneath his breath, he returned to feeling its surface. His ears awaited any sound, however slight; he would turn and act without delay. A square box on the wall brought some relief. He felt two light switches.

The first one did nothing.

The second produced a *click* from above him.

Turning around, he saw fluorescent tubes illuminating a section of the warehouse. The light lit roughly half of the room, while darkness still reigned on the opposite side. It wasn't perfect, but it felt better than having part of his view obscured.

Jared tossed the goggles to the floor, hoping the sound would encourage any vampires out from the dark.

Everything remained still.

The large room presented an ominous picture. There were rows of shelves everywhere he looked. Though empty, they were hard to see behind, especially those retreating into the shadows. Jared decided he'd inspect the area under the light first, hopeful his appearance would draw anything out that might be taking cover.

Gunfire came from behind, but Jared didn't look back. He knew Tim had run into one of the vampires and could only hope that he would take care of it. Feeling his finger twitch near the trigger of his weapon, Jared tried to calm himself. He needed to be able to hear any sound. He needed to remain focused. A flicker of light on one of the shelves on the border of the shadowed section caught his attention. Jared headed down an aisle near it, an aisle that still had some light.

Flanked by shelves on either side, he felt some comfort. It would be difficult for one of the vampires to jump on him through the obstacles. At least he had some type of warning if they attempted it. If they came on either side of the aisle, he wouldn't hesitate to pull the trigger.

The light on the shelf moved as he neared.

Jared looked behind him, trying to figure out what could be causing the reflection. Nothing stood out. When he turned back, the fragment of light danced, almost in a circle. Trying not to overreact, he leaned forward and peered into the next aisle. A shadow moved in his peripheral vision, and heavy feet dragged across the dirty floor next to him.

The vampire was in his aisle.

Jared turned, readying the gun.

He was too slow. The short, stocky male vampire was already within striking distance. It was carrying a pipe with a bent, sharpened edge. Jared lifted the gun to try and shield against the coming impact, but the edge of the pipe caught him on the right side of the face. Heat exploded as the hard object left his cheek.

Searing pain came next.

Jared's view distorted.

He opened fire.

Bullets found the vampire's throat, sending charcoal-colored gunk and skin spewing into the air. The vampire fell backward onto the floor, but Jared kept firing. Chunks of blackened guts flew all around him as he shredded the core of the vampire. Only when the gun was empty did he release the trigger. The pain returned to his face.

He tossed the gun, exchanging it for the stake, which he drove into the vampire's chest. Jared wasn't sure if he had connected with the heart, so he kept stabbing. He lost count as delirium set in.

He stopped when he saw a piece of flesh stuck on the edge of the pipe lying on the floor. Peering closer through his narrow view, he realized what it was. His right eye was looking up at him.

The vampire had ripped it out with the one swing it had managed. Nausea boiled within Jared's core, and he shuffled backward as the pain and dizziness threatened to send him into a state of unconsciousness. He placed his free hand over the hole that had once been his eye, while tears streaked down from his remaining sight organ. A mixture of emotions fought within him. Fear, anger, and sadness were but a few.

Jared willed action upon himself. Forcing his body upright, he stood, trying to survey the world around him. It wasn't easy; the light seemed dimmer, the shadows darker, and his view narrower. His own warm blood ran down the side of his face. The copper smell fought the stench of the deceased vampire for ascendancy.

A growl came from a far corner of the room.

The nightmare wasn't over.

* * *

Jared wondered if his aunt was alone, sitting and watching television as she waited for him to return home, or if she had gone out to see one of her friends. He hoped the latter. It seemed a strange time to worry about his aunt, but he did. There was no way she could run the store by herself, but what really worried him was when she looked at the finances and discovered the cruel truth. Not only would she be a widow, not only would she have to bury Jared if he found his mortal end in the godforsaken warehouse, but she'd also have to face the fact that the business was a failure. All the years of sacrifice had seen the business barely provide sustenance, waiting for its boom, which never came and never would. Jared decided that if he got out of this predicament, he'd tell his aunt the truth. They would find another way to get by.

His grip on the stake was tight. Something lurked behind a section of shelves draped in darkness to his right. His face throbbed all over his right side, but Jared pressed past the pain as he dragged his feet forward. The dusty floor assisted movement. Something scraped ahead of him. Something that was willing to enter the light to get to him. He had to move faster and surprise the vampire, as he was too easy a target at his cumbersome pace.

Biting down on his bottom lip, he propelled himself forward. This triggered more movement from behind the shelves. Shadows reached for him and a hunched figure came out from the darkness. It was the skinny old man with the long silver beard who sat nearest to him when he first met the Silverfields Nightlight Society. The man's face was now so translucent that purple-and-pink splotches appeared to hover on the surface of the skin. The outline of his skull was visible.

"Fuck you, you ugly piece of shit," Jared said, stumbling forward.

The vampire ran at him.

The speed at which the decayed-looking abomination moved was impressive. Jared no longer had the reassurance of the rifle, and his sight failed him, but he did have the stake. He roared as the vampire growled at him. Having no intention of going down without a fight, he launched himself at his opponent with all his might. Sharp teeth pierced his flesh, but Jared ignored the stinging pain in his forearm. He drove the stake into the vampire's face, ripping away skin and flesh, leaving a hole where a nose would once have been. The pale beast growled, shifted back, and then lunged for his neck.

Jared jumped forward and drove the stake into the vampire's chest. The momentum of both combatants created a powerful embrace. Inky gunk poured like a river, running free from the foe's chest. The evil creature gurgled like a drowning animal, flapping his arms over his chest.

Jared removed the stake.

The vampire dropped to the floor before him.

It didn't move.

The pain in Jared's eye and arm seemed to dissipate. A peculiar numbness moved from his extremities to his chest. Even the echo of gunfire couldn't bring him from the trancelike state that his body embraced. His view grew hazy as if fog had invaded his surroundings. His feet felt light, and for a moment Jared thought he stepped on the surface of the moon. His body tipped forward.

Darkness overwhelmed.

* * *

Confusion reigned. Jared felt as if he were waking from a deep sleep, except he couldn't pass that final threshold to reenter reality. There was tightness around one of his arms, and a voice echoed in the background. He forced his eye open.

Tim was kneeling above him. "Wake up, damn it. Wake up."

Jared was about to mumble that he was awake when Tim slapped him across the face. The sting on his cheek was brief, but it kicked his nerves back into action. The pain from wounds to his face and arm returned.

"Ah, fuck, fuck," Jared screamed. "It bit my arm."

"Good, you're alive," Tim said. "Oh yeah, I cut off your arm."

"What? My arm what?"

"I cut it off. It's not as definite as in the movies, but there was a chance you could turn. So, I needed to be sure. But don't worry, no matter what happens, at least you won't become one of them. I injected you with something for the pain. It should help a bit. I also managed to tie my belt around what's left of your arm, which should slow the bleeding."

"Holy shit, my arm," Jared said, turning his head. The horrific truth hit him like a pickup smashing into a pedestrian on a winter's day. "It's gone?"

"Yes, I already told you that. Come on, there isn't time."

"I'm fucked. I'm fucked. I'm fff—"

Tim slapped him. "Pull yourself together. This isn't over."

"What? Where are they?" Jared asked, trying not to black out again at the sight of his maimed arm. He also saw the large bloodied blade Tim had used to remove the limb. He turned to the other side and gagged.

"Looks like you got two of them. I got two as well. Just Alexander's left now."

Jared felt something cold and hard in his remaining hand.

"Here are the keys to the lock on the elevator. Take them. Get out of here. You've done your part. I put your cash, plus an extra hundred, in your back pocket. I'll find Alexander."

Jared nodded, thinking that Tim had lost his mind if he thought he cared about the money. The son of a bitch had lured him into the job. He'd cost him his eye and his arm. At least he hadn't left him to the vampires as intended, but still, he had forced this bullshit situation on him when everybody else was enjoying Labor Day, all happy and safe. Having to work sucked. If he hadn't needed the cash, he would never have been in this shithole. He pushed away further thoughts as the idea of escape came to the fore.

It wasn't until Tim helped him up that Jared realized what a mission exiting the building would be. Shuffling to the passageway, he glanced back. Tim was heading into the shadows of the warehouse. A bout of dizziness threatened to send Jared back to the cold, grimy floor. He braced through the rocking, found equilibrium, and continued on, eventually making his way down the passageway. He hoped it would be the last time he had to endure its narrow walls.

The warehouse remained silent as he left.

The lock provided another challenge. Not only because Jared had one hand left, but also because he kept fighting varying waves of disorientation and pain. Successful, he entered the elevator, and up he went.

Exiting the warehouse, he stumbled into the cool night air. He walked along the side of the building, only to succumb to a vicious wave of dizziness as he reached the front. He crawled farther and soon found himself in the middle of the road in front of the building.

No sounds came from the hellish place.

Lights, however, flowed across the road ahead of him. The screeching of tires stung his ears, and then a voice came. It was a voice he knew.

"Fuck it, man. What are you doing in the middle of the road? I could've killed you."

Jared tried to reply, but no words came out.

Footsteps approached.

"Holy shit. Jared, is that you? What the fuck happened?"

Jared rolled onto his side. His friend Lee was running toward him.

"Shit, who the fuck attacked you? Your arm is... fuck. Your eye..." Lee gripped Jared's shoulders. "Come on, stay with me. I got to get you to the hospital."

Lee managed to get him into the backseat of his car. Jared fought returning spells of disorientation until a box of spray cans held his view.

Lee slammed the car door.

"Holy shit," Lee said, getting into the driver's seat. "Your aunt tried to call you, but you left your phone at home. She sent me here to find you. You circled this ad on a newspaper in your room."

Lee started up the engine. Jared felt his head sway.

His vision turned murky.

Gunshots echoed in the distance.

"What the fuck is going on?" Lee asked, pulling away.

Jared knew Tim was responsible for the shots. He had no doubt run into Alexander. Tim would finish him off, sending the stake through the vampire's heart after showering him with bullets. Tim, the man he barely knew, who had apparently been serving vampires hidden in the shadows of Jared's hometown. Tim, who had grown tired of being in their servitude. Tim would end the vampires' reign in Silverfields and bury the secret. There were many questions swirling in Jared's head, but he doubted he'd get any answers.

Black spots danced in his view.

Even the pain seemed to have given up trying to keep him awake.

"Hang on, Jared, just hang on," Lee said, banging the steering wheel. "Hey, buddy, listen. Listen to me. Your aunt got a call from some investors this evening. They want to buy the store and the two next door. She wanted to talk to you urgently because they require a meeting with all the owners tomorrow. The other owners have already agreed. She said the fee they're offering is incredible. You guys are going to be fine. You can live your life. You hear me? Jared?"

Jared had heard. His aunt would be fine. He tried to ignore the copper smell coming out of his mouth when he exhaled. It didn't help that every time he inhaled a sharp pain darted across his chest. The darkness drew nearer. Jared didn't know what it wanted, what it meant, or where it would lead him, but he no longer had the energy to fight.

"Jared? We're almost at the hospital. You hear me? Bud?"

Jared shut his eye.

"Jared? Answer me, Goddammit!"

His aunt would be fine.

"Jared?"

The nightmare of the warehouse was over.

TRICK OR DEATH

Once Barry Steiner knocked, there would be no going back. He glanced over his shoulder, scanning the neighborhood one last time. There was no activity, except for the towering streetlights with their flickering pale beams fighting back encroaching black shadows. The darkness was good. The darkness would help. He had picked the right time and the perfect place to start.

He breathed in slowly as he reached the faded white door.

He gripped the weapon he held in his other hand, hoping the mask he wore covered every inch of his face. His free hand formed a fist, and he knocked.

A chair creaked inside.

Labored footsteps approached.

Barry ducked into a shadowy area on the porch. He lifted the weapon above his waist as his heart beat like the drums in a heavy metal song. Excitement and fear dueled within him, sending sparks of energy up and down his limbs. He had to move fast. Speed would be key.

The front door opened, and the illumination within highlighted a box-shaped section of the porch. The light fell over the front edge of the cloak Barry wore, but it didn't matter. It was too late for this person, even if he or she caught a glimpse of him.

"Hello, anyone there?" an elderly woman asked. Her silver-gray curls barely moved as she turned her head from side to side. "Damn kids. You don't want your candy, do you then?"

Barry recognized the woman. She was his first intended victim.

He jumped from his hiding spot, waving the scythe that came with the Grim Reaper Halloween costume pack. "Trick or death?" Barry asked, trying to keep his voice deep and rough.

"Oh, oh," Miss Isabel Grady said, raising her hands in front of her face. She let out a high-pitched scream that would have made a banshee proud.

"Your time has come, Miss Grady."

"You—you son of a bitch. You scared the crap out of me."

Barry's core shook, and laughter escaped his throat. Miss Grady's reaction had been pure gold, from the gaping mouth to the wavering voice, and then the frenetic movement of her hands.

There was no doubt he had frightened her. Barry made the perfect Grim Reaper, and he was glad he hadn't skimped when purchasing the costume. He wore the long black cloak, the skull mask, and held the plastic scythe, but it had also come with a pair of skeleton-hand gloves to complete the transformation. People couldn't see his curly black hair or his skinny frame beneath the cloak, two of his features people teased him about.

"Who the hell are you? Take that damn mask off," Miss Grady said. Her lips pursed.

Barry removed the mask. "It's me, Miss Grady. Barry Steiner."

"Barry, what on earth are you doing? You're too old to be trick-or-treating."

"I'm sorry, Miss Grady. I'm shooting some footage for my YouTube channel. Is it cool if I use your reaction?"

"Um, well, okay, but wait," Miss Grady said. Her face had returned to its normal color. "I think I swore. Did I swear? You can't use it if I did."

"I can edit it out. No problem at all."

"Oh, okay, well fine then." Miss Grady waved her hand at him. "Now get out of here. What's wrong with you?"

"Thanks." Barry flashed a smile. "Good night, Miss Grady."

The front door closed.

Barry turned and gave a bush alongside Miss Grady's home the thumbs-up. "All right," he said, grinning, "you can come out of hiding."

Rose Garcia, his friend since childhood, appeared from behind the bush. In one hand she held a digital camera, and with the other, she reciprocated the thumbs-up. Barry figured that meant she had recorded the prank without a hitch, but her face didn't look happy. He tried attributing the look of agitation he saw to the poor lighting. Miss Grady's reaction was just too good; he needed to make sure the footage was clear, even if it meant opening himself up for a sharp remark from Rose.

"Did you record her reaction?" Barry asked.

"Duh, Barry. What's your next stupid question? Can I count to three?"

Barry smiled.

Halloween night was off to a fantastic start.

* * *

Barry had planned the night's activities when he grew frustrated with the lull in growth of some of his social media accounts, particularly his YouTube channel. He wanted more subscribers. He needed more likes. Brainstorming had brought forth possibilities like reaction-and-review videos about popular music and movies or maybe even some tips-and-technique videos on subjects he knew well, but those ideas failed to excite him. Then an idea came, one that caused static electricity to erupt all over his body.

He would do pranks.

Barry parked a safe distance from house number two, a small white cottage. It was peculiar for the street, but not when you knew about its owner, Polly Cutler. She had served behind the counter at the local post office for decades and was known for her eccentric dress sense and ever-changing hair color. Retired now, she'd most likely spend the days tending to her garden.

Walking toward the front door, Barry made a note to watch his step. The last thing he wanted was to trample any of her beloved plants. He inhaled the earthy aroma of the garden as he checked his sides for any activity. The block was silent; no kids had found their way out here yet. Most of them started their trick-or-treating from the center of town outward until they had enough candy to feast upon. Barry pointed for Rose to hide behind a large black trash can on the side of the house. She would have to zoom in a bit, and he hoped she would know how.

Barry knocked.

He ducked behind a rack of hanging flowers. The cover was poor, but all he needed was a second to jump out. A light above the front door came on, exposing him.

"Shit," he muttered, dropping onto his haunches and trying to scoot behind a potted plant near the front door.

The door opened.

"Hello," Polly said, holding a bowl of sweets before her. "Hello, is anyone there? I heard the knock."

Barry jumped up from his spot. "Trick or death?"

Polly swung the bowl at him, sending sweets flying in every direction like shrapnel from a bomb blast. She gasped and then tried to grab the scythe from Barry. He moved, dodging her lunge.

"Grrrrr, I've come for you. It's your time," he growled.

Polly screamed, punching in his direction. The blow hit Barry on the right cheek. It carried enough force to cause him to flinch. Barry had heard that when people were in fearful situations, the adrenaline could give them a boost in strength. Fortunately, Polly didn't deliver another strike. She turned around and dashed into her house.

She banged the door shut.

Trying to speak past the pain in his jaw, Barry said, "Miss Cutler, it's a joke. It's just a joke."

Polly didn't answer.

"Miss Cutler, it was a little prank. It's a video for my channel. Would you mind if I use your reaction? Hey... Miss Cutler?"

"Get out of here," she shouted from the newfound safety behind the door. "Or I'm calling the cops."

Barry removed the mask and made his way to the car, cursing beneath his breath. He shook his head as Rose caught up to him. "Shit, that would have been a great one. Now I'll have to blur out her face or something. What bullshit, huh?"

Rose handed him the camera. "Listen, Barry. What do you say we end this and go to my place?"

"Say what?"

"Let's talk in the car."

* * *

In the car, Rose's citrus-scented perfume tickled Barry's nostrils. He turned to her. She was frowning, looking out the passenger window. Barry sensed he might not like what she had to say. If Rose needed to think about her words, they generally weren't "well done" or "great job." Her black hair, flowing down her shoulders, bounced as she turned to him.

"What did you want to talk about?" Barry asked.

"This is kinda childish."

"What? What are you talking about? You agreed with me all week that it was a cool idea."

Rose shook her head. "I only said that because I thought it was what you wanted to hear. But we're too old for this nonsense. And Barry, there's something else I need to tell you."

She moved closer. "How long have we known each other?"

"Ah, since we were kids. Duh," he said.

"Barry, I like you. Do you truly believe I'm out here because I want to roam the neighborhood, scaring a bunch of old people?"

"I like you too, Rose. But shit, you could've told me you thought the idea sucked. There's no need to attack me now." Barry looked at the mask in his hand. Suddenly it did seem a little stupid.

"No, Barry, you're not hearing me. I don't just like you as a friend. I really, really like you. Get it? I've felt this way for a while now."

The words hit harder than Miss Cutler's punch, as they came with the force of a baseball bat connecting on a home-run swing—clean, powerful, and with a *crack*. It dawned on him with the same life-altering effect fire must have had on cavemen. He was on the cusp of having Rose as a girlfriend. The sudden revelation of her feelings for him forced introspection. It had been a long time since he'd considered Rose as more than a friend. Not because he didn't like her that way, but because he'd never believed she would ever reciprocate his feelings. Everything had changed in the space of a few seconds.

Rose leaned forward and kissed him. Her tongue danced in his mouth. For a moment Barry forgot who he was, or where he was.

Rose pulled away. "Let's go back to my place. If you want to be with me as more than just a friend, stop the childish nonsense. It's time to grow up. The silly antics need to stop."

Conflicting emotions, like two kids fighting over one game controller, battled within him. He wanted to go with Rose. He wanted to be with Rose. Yet, he also wanted to have new footage for his channel. Two clips wouldn't cut it. All the planning, the cost of getting the costume, and the perfect start and footage at Miss Grady's would be all for nothing.

He carefully considered his words.

"Rose, I really like you too. I've been crazy about you for as long as I can remember. But I need to finish this tonight, and then I swear I'll move on. I'll do product reviews and reactions. Hell, I'll even do ASMR. You know, popular stuff like that. I swear."

Rose frowned.

"Wait, wait," Barry said, realizing he was losing. Rose's lips tightened; she was getting annoyed. "Okay, just one more house and one more scare. They say good things happen in threes, right? I wanted to get the doc before ending the pranks. He's always great. You know that."

"Who says good things come in threes?" Rose shrugged. "But okay. Tell you what," she said, looking at her phone. "I'm going home. If you don't rock up within forty-five minutes, I'm going to bed. Do you understand what I'm saying?"

"Yeah, but who will hold the camera?"

Rose climbed out of the vehicle and walked away, ignoring his question. "Better make that forty-four minutes."

"Hang on," Barry said, getting out and running after her.

"Here." He handed her the car keys. "You drive home. I don't want you walking alone at night. I'll run to the doc's and then head straight for your place."

"You sure? Your time is running out."

"I'm sure."

"Fine."

"Wait. Can I get another kiss? For luck?"

Rose stepped to him but didn't lean forward with her face. Instead, she wrapped her arms around him, giving him a brief hug.

"We'll see if you want another kiss." She turned around and headed for the vehicle.

She lived ten minutes away from the doc, quicker if Barry ran. He didn't like having to do the prank alone. However, the realization that Rose was going to be his girlfriend heartened him.

Barry started jogging when he heard Rose fire up the engine.

He would scare the doc shitless and head over to her with time to spare. He would have some footage for his channel, and he would have Rose. No man throughout the history of time had a night that could compete with his amazing Halloween.

It was the stuff of dreams.

* * *

House number three was a bit farther up the road from Polly's. It was a fancy two-story home with a stone path, flanked by flowers on one side and a pond on the other. There was even a little bridge that ran over the pond if you wanted to take a detour to a wooden bench beneath the stars. This house belonged to Doctor Rudy Lambert, one of the local medical practitioners. He had treated Barry on many occasions. Scaring the good doc was only fair considering all the injections he'd received from the man when growing up.

Disappointment dug a hole in Barry's stomach, however. All the lights were off. Blackness held the home firmly in its grip. Realizing he had time, Barry hoped there was someone around even if all the evidence suggested otherwise. He marched to the white front door, set the camera up, and selected Record, hoping to catch any reaction.

He pressed the doorbell's button.

It made no sound.

Barry found it odd that the doctor, a wealthy man compared to many in town, would have a broken doorbell. The pull of leaving and going to Rose strengthened like the undertow of an ocean's current, and if he didn't knock within five seconds, he would pack it in. Five, four... The seconds counted down in his head as a dreamy vision of Rose's lips appeared in the fore of his mind. Three... Two... Then came a sharper image of a boost in his subscribers and likes, so many likes. One...

Barry knocked.

No footsteps approached.

The door didn't open.

He heard something rattle and scrape, almost as if someone were moving a set of keys over a wooden surface. Intrigue sparked within him. Could it be that Doctor Lambert was trying to hide out from Halloween? Maybe he was sitting in a dimmed-out room to avoid the neighborhood kids? It seemed unlike the good doc, which only made Barry more curious about the reason behind the sound. Time was still on Barry's side, and an idea came to him.

He made his way around the house, opening the black iron gate on the side carefully so as not to make any sound. Doctor Lambert didn't own a dog, thus, there was no reason for fear, but he didn't want to alert anyone of his moves. He simply refused to give up on his scare, especially from a man hiding from Halloween. That was unforgivable. Barry decided he would knock at least three times before surrendering.

He set up the camera, knocked on the back door, and then hid. No sounds came, so he tried knocking again, louder this time.

Nothing happened.

The frustration caused an itch to break out all over his neck. He had endured enough and no longer cared to knock a third time. The damn doc could hide if he wanted. Barry had better things to do.

He grabbed the camera, noticing a thin bar of light escaping from what looked like an air vent near the bottom of the back door. The doc had a basement and was probably chilling on a recliner, laughing at Barry's knocking, thinking he was getting one over on some kids. This infuriated Barry because his victim wasn't simply hiding; he was getting a kick out of Barry's frustration.

Barry walked to the back door, knowing instantly that Rose would disapprove of his next move. She wasn't here, though, and what she didn't know couldn't hurt him.

He tried the handle.

Unlocked.

It didn't occur to Barry that he was breaking and entering until he stood in the dark kitchen, checking the camera. Surely nothing could go wrong. He'd give the old doc a scare and then quickly announce who he was. Doctor Lambert would see the funny side of the prank. With the newfound confidence gained from Rose's declaration of her feelings for him, this all made perfect sense.

He was untouchable. He was the man.

Just before the living room, he saw a door with light escaping beneath it. The basement. His assumption of the doc hiding away was true. The scene reminded Barry of ones he had watched in horror films growing up, but he braced himself, allowing the initial tickle of fear to move on. This time he knew what to expect. There were no monsters or other horrors awaiting him. He imagined Doctor Lambert sitting in pajamas, drinking beer, and laughing to himself as Halloween passed on by around him.

Barry grinned beneath the mask and turned the brass ball handle.

* * *

The stairs had been surprisingly quiet to traverse. They were either new or hadn't endured too many feet. They didn't lead to an open room with a big screen, a recliner, and a bar fridge. Nor did they lead to a room filled with dusty shelves and old appliances or even boxes. No, before Barry was another door. Surely the doc was relaxing behind it.

Barry ran his hand over its cold surface.

He got the camera ready and then turned the handle.

The door opened heavily.

A sharp white light greeted him. He launched himself into the room, swinging the camera around, not wanting to miss capturing his victim's petrified face.

"Your time has come, good doctor," Barry said in a deep, forced voice while searching the room. "Death is here."

He didn't see anyone. Then, someone groaned.

The sound reminded him of a person awaking from a deep sleep and trying to find their bearings. Barry couldn't ascertain where the sound came from, and his initial idea of the room proved incorrect. There was no chair to relax in, no fridge for the beers, and no doc in pajamas.

He removed the mask he wore. The jig was up one way or another.

The room had no windows, but there was the one small air vent he'd already seen. It had steel bars over it. A desk covered with old PC parts and some kid's science kit stood ahead of him. The wall to his left was full of circular lights behind a large, round, nearly see-through cover. Taking a step closer, he noticed some sections of the cover had a type of gray paint splashed over them, giving the illusion of shadows. The whole image looked familiar... The creation mimicked the dominant celestial body in our night sky, the moon. The image of the body that controlled the ocean currents caused a moment of concern within him.

"Barry Steiner," a hoarse, female voice said, "what are you doing here?"

Barry turned to see a figure crawl out from the side of the desk, almost as if she had been hiding to avoid the illumination in the room. "Miss Lambert, is that you?"

"You must leave, Barry. Now."

"What? Why? I'm sorry for barging in. I was just trying to do some pranks tonight," Barry said, sure the person was indeed Doctor Lambert's sister, Angela Lambert. She had often assisted at the doctor's practice in the early days, usually as the receptionist. He remembered her clearly because whenever he'd finished with a visit, she would always give him a hug before wishing him well. Sometimes she had even given him an extra sweet from behind the counter.

Angela looked sluggish, ill perhaps.

"Are you okay?" Barry asked.

Angela got to her feet. There were chains attached to her arms, preventing her from taking more than three steps toward Barry. "You must leave before my brother comes. We are testing tonight. He is helping me with my condition but does not want anyone else to know."

"What are you talking about?"

"You must go. Now, Barry."

"Too late," a deep voice said.

Barry turned around. A man stood in the doorway, hidden by the shadows of the staircase. A burst of static came from Barry's side. He turned and saw a grainy image on a black-and-white television screen on the wall. A green light blinked next to the screen. The screen was a feed from a security camera placed at the front door of the house. He saw who was pressing the broken doorbell, except it wasn't broken. It set off the green light.

"Rose," he whispered.

"Looks like we have another visitor," the man said. "I'd better go see to it. Hopefully, they move along. Good thing I locked the back. Wouldn't want another one sneaking in while I run an errand."

Barry turned to the man leaving. There was a device in the man's hand that flashed a green light like the one next to the screen.

"Wait," Barry shouted, making for the doorway.

The man didn't.

Barry reached out with his left arm, hoping to stop the man from closing the door. The man's voice still echoed in his head, and with certainty he determined whom it belonged to. Yes, it was Doctor Lambert, but why was he acting so strange? Was it a Halloween prank? Had the tables turned on him? Barry couldn't be sure, and in his panic, he dropped the camera. It cracked as it landed on the hard floor.

Doctor Lambert swung the door closed.

Barry didn't have time to move his arm out of the way, and the door slammed his arm against the frame, above his wrist. The door didn't bounce back as expected, and a waft of stale air slapped him in the face. The door had shut. It wasn't possible. Barry could still see his arm barring the door from closing. An escalating pain and a strange burning sensation crawled around his wrist; he pulled his arm back.

His left hand was gone.

Blood spurted from the severed limb.

Grogginess infiltrated him, almost as if he had taken one too many sleeping pills. The door was no ordinary one keeping him from exiting the basement. There must be a sharpened metal edge, blade or—

Barry blacked out.

* * *

As Barry came to, a sharp pain sent spikes of flaming heat up his arm. The world seemed shaky, as if the Earth rocked on its axis or an asteroid attack pounded away at the planet. Either way, none of that would matter if he didn't stem the bleeding. He wasn't sure how long he'd been out for, but he doubted it had been too long, as his arm was still losing blood with a healthy flow. Crawling back into the center of the room, he noticed the wooden floor had scratches all over its surface.

"Miss Lambert? Angela? I need your help. Please..." Barry said. "Your psycho brother chopped off my hand."

Angela crouched in the corner. "No, no, not now, not now, please not now. I am so sorry," she mumbled. "I never wanted anyone to get hurt."

"She's lucky, that Rose," a tinny voice said from an old wooden speaker high on the wall. "She knocked, and then carried on up the road, unlike you, who just had to be so nosy. She looked a bit disappointed when she walked away. Hope she wasn't expecting you anytime soon."

"Fuck you, you sick fucker," Barry said, realizing it was the doc. "Now let me out of this—"

A large, dusty, incandescent red light started blinking on the wall.

Doctor Lambert didn't reply.

"You must go," Angela said. "I can't stop it."

"What the fuck are you talking about?"

The lights on the wall mimicking the moon burst with a sudden newfound brightness behind the circular cover. Barry shielded his eyes with his remaining hand, fearful the potent white light would burn his eyes.

He turned to Angela.

"What's going on?" Barry asked, trying to rip off a piece of his costume to tie around his arm. A moment of dizziness rattled his head. He braced through it, trying to remain calm. "Goddamn it, Angela, tell me."

"I'm turning," she said. "The chains won't hold me. Only the room is strong enough to keep me in."

"Huh? I don't understand," Barry said. Tying the piece of costume around his arm was proving difficult.

Angela didn't reply. A deafening howl sent shivers down Barry's spine. He looked up. A type of hairy animal—no, a beast—had replaced Angela. Her clothes now lay torn on the floor. The creature had a long mouth with a pitch-black snout at its end. Sharp, dirty canine teeth appeared when it snarled at him. Suddenly it all made sense: the basement, the steel door, the chains, even the one air vent with its steel bars. All these precautions were to keep something in and not to keep intruders out.

A werewolf.

A fucking *werewolf*.

The Angela Lambert he knew was gone. A nightmare had replaced the good-natured and caring receptionist in town who gave kids hugs and extra sweets when they saw the doctor. He remembered Angela would always promise everything would be fine when he visited the doc. He had always believed her.

This time no promise in the world would convince Barry all would be fine.

The werewolf growled as it snapped free from the chains. Its power and speed caused Barry to flinch. There was no way he could match the animal. It turned its neck, surveying him. Yellow eyes with narrow black pupils yearned for the prey locked in their sight.

The eyes promised nothing but pain and death, yet the beast didn't charge. The nightmare didn't launch for him. It simply strolled over to Barry and lifted him.

It embraced him like grandparents hugging grandkids they hadn't seen in a while. Except this creature's hold didn't cease, and it tightened when it should have eased. He could smell the stench of ammonia and blood as his senses heightened. He shook as the fear coursed through his veins with the temperature of Arctic water, while the werewolf tightened its grip.

A loud *crack* came from the middle of the pair's embrace.

The sound came from within Barry. A bone inside his body had snapped.

"Holy shit," Barry screamed. "Please...please stop."

The werewolf's grip tightened like a vice.

Crack, snap, crack, pop, crack, snap. The symphony of destruction within reached a crescendo as his ribs and other bones gave way to the force. There were burning sensations, and sharp, piercing spikes, with jolts of pain accompanying the orchestra of hurt. Barry knew the internal damage was beyond repair. Internal bleeding, crushed organs, severed muscles, ripped nerves, and pierced skin would be just a bit of the damage to go with the multiple fractures.

He couldn't breathe. His mind searched for a spot, any spot, where there was no pain. It found none. The night had begun so well, from the perfect first reaction, to the possibility of a relationship with Rose. Why hadn't he listened? Everything would have been so different. It all hit Barry as another bone cracked in his arm.

He didn't just like Rose. He loved her. He *fucking* loved her.

The werewolf released him, and he collapsed on the floor.

The last sound he heard was the beast's howl.

THANKS SINNING

It all started with a glass shattering.

Screaming followed, angry words wrapped in an extra layer of hate. At first they sounded distant, as if they had traversed the space from a parallel universe. DeShawn Williams realized they weren't from aliens hell-bent on our destruction. No, these words came from fellow humans, the ones right behind his table in the local bar. A tall man with a pitch-black survivalist beard, wearing a checkered shirt and a green trucker cap, was pointing his finger at a young platinum-blonde haired server. She wore a white shirt with a crooked blue name tag and reciprocated the man's pointed index finger with her middle finger.

The man snarled and stomped his foot. "You fucking bitch. You won't get away with this. Trevor was fine until he met you. Now he can barely string two sentences together."

"I told him I wasn't interested in a relationship. We had one night of fun. And then he wouldn't leave me alone."

"Absolute bullshit. Trevor has a beautiful wife, you wannabe home-wrecker. Why would he waste his time chasing a freak like you?"

The woman slapped the man. The connection of hand to face sounded like the *crack* of a whip. Lifting his hand, the man threatened to return the action. Before he could, a burly, bald bouncer, dressed in black from head to toe, stepped between them. The bouncer pointed to the man. "You. Get out, now."

He turned to the woman. "And, you, boss wants to see you in the back."

DeShawn returned his view to the empty beer glass in front of him. Life after college wasn't going the way he had planned. With his father over in Iraq, considering extending his military duty by an additional six months, DeShawn had to stay at home to keep an eye on his mother and younger sister. He wanted to move away and explore, live his own life, but remained chained to the hometown he already knew too well.

He looked up at the highlights from a college football game on an overhead screen. Watching the game unfold brought him no real enjoyment, but it felt odd not to have any responsibilities, if even for a brief time. It was nice to be able to sit and not have to run from one errand to the next, from problem to problem.

"Another drink?" a female voice asked.

DeShawn looked at the beautiful woman with short raven black hair. She wore a black tank top, tight dark denims, and heels. Her face looked familiar, and as she tried to peer behind the curtain of his mind with her dark green eyes, he realized who she was.

"Wait, you're the server . . . from just now? The one involved in the argument?"

"Very perceptive. The blonde wig gets more tips. Mind if I take a seat?"

She didn't wait for his reply and sat in the red-cushioned chair opposite him, placing her dark purple handbag on the table. After retrieving a pack of smokes, she lit one, inhaled deeply, and exhaled the pale gray smoke into the air.

"Ah, so you work here often? I haven't seen you around." DeShawn wanted a sip from his beer, hoping the alcohol would aid his confidence. Before he grabbed it, he remembered it was empty.

"Worked," the woman said. "I'm done with this place, these people. Life is too short to put up with this shit."

"Yeah, I hear that. I'm DeShawn, by the way." DeShawn held out his hand.

The woman didn't shake his hand; she took a drag on her cigarette. She glanced around the bar, shaking her head as if nothing caught her interest. While guiding the cigarette back to her mouth, she paused, lowered her hand, and rested the cigarette above the ashtray. She looked at DeShawn.

"Say, you look like fun. What do you say we get out of here? It is Thanksgiving, after all. We should be out enjoying what little time we have in this realm. Don't you agree?"

DeShawn couldn't go with her. Family expected him home for Thanksgiving in less than an hour. What of his needs, though? Didn't he deserve the chance to do something spontaneous? Get away from all the shit in his life? No, he had to go home. He searched for an excuse. Honesty, he figured, would be the easiest and best route. She'd understand.

"Um, listen," DeShawn said.

The woman leaned forward, and her facial features softened as if she knew what was coming. She reached out with her hand. DeShawn instinctively reciprocated with his, and they shook. Her skin felt soft, warm, and then she smiled. Suddenly, DeShawn wasn't as concrete in his decision to go home.

"I'm Lucy, Lucy Fern, by the way." She rubbed her thumb over his knuckles. "It's nice to meet you, DeShawn."

"Nice to meet you, too."

Lucy signaled for one of the servers and ordered two shots of tequila.

"Here." She took out a black wallet, liberated a few notes from it, and then slid it to DeShawn. "Put this in one of your pockets."

"What? Why?"

"They won't search you."

"Whose is it?"

"Well, DeShawn. It belongs to the asshole who was having a fight with me. I want to teach him a lesson." Lucy put the palms of her hands together as if she were in prayer. "You're gonna help me, right? It's not okay for a man to speak to a woman that way. You agree, don't you?"

DeShawn took the wallet. Being around Lucy made it seem as though it wasn't technically wrong. His conscience reminded him that he was incorrect, and that it was stealing, but he didn't care. He had heard what the man said. Maybe Lucy was right, and the man needed a lesson. It was the first time DeShawn could recall stealing since being a kid and taking sweets from his local store with some of his friends. Maybe taking the wallet would cause him to feel something else other than the despair of the last few months.

"Thank you," Lucy said. "Oh, and I already checked. There's about eighty dollars left in the wallet. You can have it."

DeShawn nodded. There was still no spike in his emotions concerning the wallet, but when Lucy said 'thank you,' a nervous energy had circled in his stomach.

The server brought the tequilas. Lucy paid and wasted no time downing her drink. Not wanting to look like a nerd, DeShawn followed suit. All the while he couldn't break free from the feeling that he had to get going. The monotony of home life awaited him. A part of his mind was trying to find reasons to justify going with Lucy. It was so different being around her. She made him forget the shit hand life had dealt him. Moreover, she was beautiful, and she was interested in being around him. Would it be so bad if he rocked up home a bit late?

"Do you enjoy sex?" Lucy asked.

DeShawn cleared his throat. "Um, yeah, of course."

"Good, so do I. I haven't gotten laid in over a week." Lucy's soft pink lips formed a smile. Her eyes mesmerized beneath the lights of the bar. "Come on, let's get out of here."

DeShawn had come to a decision.

He would be arriving home late for Thanksgiving.

* * *

Lucy's breasts swayed hypnotically before DeShawn as she straddled him, grinding against his crotch. She'd guided him to a cabin outside of town. To DeShawn's surprise, Lucy had told him this was where she stayed. That was all a fading memory. She leaned forward, her breasts brushing over his face.

DeShawn reached for her purple G-string, the last piece of clothing she wore.

"Wait," she said. "Before we have fun, I want you to prove that you deserve me with a little game."

"Huh?"

Lucy ignored him, got up, and retrieved her clothes lying all over the floor.

DeShawn had seen a couple of tattoos while they undressed, from a burning butterfly on her right bicep to the saying "sinning is winning" over her left wrist, but he was a little caught off guard to see that her entire back was a canvas to various images and words. As Lucy pulled up her skirt, a spider crawled from her left hip toward the middle of her back. There, it found a resting spot in one of the empty eye sockets of a large silver skull.

DeShawn shook his head and blinked. The light was dim inside the cabin. Surely the spider had been an optical illusion? Or maybe there were more of them on her back, and he had imagined he'd seen one of them move.

After pulling up his boxers, he climbed out of bed and made his way toward Lucy, never taking his gaze off her back and the spider hiding in the skull. He stopped right behind her while she fastened her bra.

"Oh, you came to help? Such a gentleman." She chuckled.

DeShawn helped her, clumsily; reminiscent of the first time he had ever helped a girl with a bra. He didn't care what Lucy thought. His focus had shifted to her left hip. There was no spider, but there was an empty spider web. It didn't make any sense.

He shouldn't have been drinking so early in the day. Clearly, he was more inebriated than he realized. Ignoring the strange illusion he had seen on Lucy's back, he collected his clothes and put them on.

Lucy came over to him, holding a glass of water in one hand while concealing something in a closed fist. "Here."

She opened her hand.

"What's that?" DeShawn asked, frowning at the sight of the large purple egg-shaped pill.

"It's just a little pick-me-up. I already took one."

"I don't do drugs."

"It's not a drug. It's natural. Been around for ages. It'll make your life a bit more interesting."

"Sounds like a drug to me."

Lucy walked away.

"Okay, okay, I'll take your pill. I trust you."

She turned around and smiled.

DeShawn swallowed the pill against his better judgment. He took a sip of the warm water as Lucy watched, hoping it was some type of natural energy pill or maybe something to sober him up. He was acting out of character today, but it had been a while coming. Having to toe the line at home for so long, he needed an escape. One day to act out, to take the paths he normally wouldn't.

"We have to go outside to play," Lucy said, making her way toward the door. "But before we go, we need to get something."

DeShawn downed the rest of the water and made his way to her. The pill had tasted bland. Had she given him a placebo to mess with him?

Lucy opened a dusty toolbox on a small wooden table by the door. She turned around and handed DeShawn a hunting knife. The weapon looked blunt and rusted, and its grip worn.

"What should I do with this?" DeShawn held the knife out before him as if it were a dirty sock.

Lucy grinned. "Hey, you never know. Maybe we'll run into a wild animal."

"And this will help?"

"Sure," Lucy said, raising her hand and revealing a hammer. "You don't mind, do you? I've always seen myself more as the hammer-wielding type."

"It's cool, I guess." A light sweat had broken out on DeShawn's forehead. He hoped it was due to the midday rise in temperature. "Let's get outside if we're going. I could use some fresh air."

Lucy merely admired her hammer.

* * *

A resplendent world bursting with a kaleidoscope of colors greeted DeShawn outside. He strolled forward, glancing to each side, waiting for his eyes to adjust to the bright lights of the outdoor world. He didn't need fresh air after all and missed Lucy's body on top of him. He wanted her warm, soft lips.

Lucy placed her hand on his shoulder for support as she took her heels off. "I want to feel the ground beneath my feet today."

She skipped barefoot ahead of him, surveying the surrounding trees. DeShawn wasn't sure what she was looking for, but when he saw her sniff the air, he became agitated.

"What are you doing?" he asked. "Let's go back inside."

"I bet you couldn't hit the bird over there." Lucy pointed her hammer at a tree near him.

"Hit a bird with this blunt blade? What? You want me to knock it out?"

"A real man could kill it with one throw."

DeShawn shrugged. He had no intention of killing a bird but figured if he threw the knife close enough, it might take flight. He hoped this would bring an end to Lucy's game, so they could get back to finishing what they had started inside. Tingling warmth had begun building from within his core.

"All right," he said. "I'll take a shot."

"Excellent," Lucy said, twirling on the spot. "You've got this. I just know it."

DeShawn located the pale blue bird on a branch and aimed to the left of it. His goal was to rattle a bunch of leaves hanging nearby. He tossed the knife, but his aim was a bit low and to the right. For a moment, a rogue branch alongside the leaves was in trouble. Gravity safely guided the blade beneath it. The knife missed everything but air. The bird remained sitting, unfazed.

"Awww, nice try. But now it's my turn," Lucy said.

She readied the hammer, and her eyes narrowed as she locked onto her target. DeShawn got the feeling she had done this many times before.

Lucy's hammer left her hand.

The bird realized its fate too late.

It fell from its branch to the earth. DeShawn turned toward Lucy, who was smiling and holding her hands up. He felt no sympathy for the bird, which was odd because he usually cared for animals. The warmth in his core had increased a notch. Disorientation passed over him as he stared at Lucy, who danced seductively.

"I won," she said. "I won."

"Can we go back in? Finish what we started?"

Lucy shook her head. The suggestive swaying of her body ceased. She walked and picked up both the hammer and the rusty knife. The dead bird no longer held any interest for her. She didn't even give it a passing glance.

"Ah, come on," DeShawn said, throwing his hands up. "Why can't we go back in?"

"You've still got to kill. I'm not doing anything until you show you're a man. But I'll find something else, something that'll really be impressive."

"We could be here all day."

Lucy smiled. "Not if you have a bigger target."

* * *

Lucy led DeShawn into the woods surrounding her cabin. The aroma of the plant life grew stronger the farther they walked. DeShawn's sight got blurrier. Tree after tree and bush after bush, it all began to look alike. The world blended into itself. There was no tether for DeShawn back to the world he knew. It was then that he realized the pill had been no placebo. It wasn't an overwhelming narcotic. Its hold was slight, as if it was guiding from behind the curtain.

"You're not going to pass out on me?" Lucy asked, twisting and breaking a branch on her right. She had a habit of breaking branches around her that weren't even in her way. She'd also smashed a spider that had been crawling on one of the tree trunks during their walk.

"No," DeShawn said.

"Good. We're almost there."

It didn't take long, and the two of them stepped into a circular clearing. The scene looked a little ominous, almost as if this part of the world had been subject to a peculiar scorched-earth policy. The air had an ashy smell to it, and the ground was bare. No grass or other foliage existed. All that remained was the darkened soil and some rocks on the clearing's perimeter. The rocks hadn't found placement at random; DeShawn could sense a design.

"This is my special place," Lucy said.

"Okay."

"Not just okay, amazing." She handed him the rusty knife. "Do you see it?"

"See what?"

"Look to your left."

DeShawn studied the line of trees at the edge of the clearing, seeking anything out of place. He was about to turn back to Lucy when he saw a large brown bag, except something wasn't right. The bag appeared to have limbs. Were they branches tricking his mind?

He moved closer. It was a person . . . a man. Someone had tied his arms and legs to the tree and taped his mouth shut. He was standing, staring back at DeShawn. With his thick, graying black beard and bloodshot eyes, he looked as though he hadn't seen home in ages. All he wore was a large and dirty brown jacket, which was what DeShawn first thought was a bag, and a pair of once-white briefs that rivaled his jacket in filth.

"What the fuck is this?" DeShawn asked.

Lucy skipped ahead of him. "It's awesome, isn't it?"

"I don't understand. What's going on?"

"That's your target."

DeShawn couldn't keep his jaw from dropping. Lucy ignored his expression. She stopped about ten paces from the man tied to the tree and waited for DeShawn to catch up to her. She pressed her hands on DeShawn's chest when he did.

"Nope," she said, shaking her head. "This is as close as you can get. Otherwise it won't be much of a challenge."

DeShawn ignored her and pushed on past, marching toward the man. Gripping the knife, he proceeded to sever the rope binding the man's arms. He nodded while he worked, trying to calm the man's groans. The rope was tough, the knife blunt. DeShawn persevered.

"What are you doing?" Lucy asked.

DeShawn ignored her again. Her beauty no longer held the appeal it had in the cabin. He clenched his teeth, focusing on the rope.

Lucy grabbed his sides, attempting to pull him away from the man. Her strength was surprising, but it wasn't enough to stop him. She punched his back, and then moved lower, targeting his kidneys. DeShawn didn't flinch. The rope had only a few stubborn strands left.

The hammer smashed into his right hand.

DeShawn dropped the knife, wincing. "What the fuck?"

Lucy didn't respond.

He bent down and grabbed the knife, determined to cut the man loose. As he stood, he realized he'd already done enough. The man had broken free from the rope, though he was crawling on the ground almost as if he'd forgotten how to walk.

"Run, dude, run," DeShawn shouted, turning to face Lucy.

"No," she commanded, readying the hammer to strike at the man.

DeShawn pushed her back with enough force that she fell onto her rear. The man was standing, and with the newfound equilibrium, he didn't waste any time. He hobbled away, disappearing into the woods.

"Why would you do that to me? To us?" Lucy got up and started bouncing on her feet like a child throwing a tantrum. "Sinning is winning. Sinning is winning. Sinning is winning."

"What is wrong with—"

"Sinning is what feeds me. Sinning is what feeds us. Don't you understand? Without it, we die. Killing him would have fed us for weeks."

"Listen, you need fucking help," DeShawn said, taking a step backward. "You're not well."

"I feel wonderful. And we can still catch him if we work together. He's nobody, a homeless beggar. I caught him sleeping behind the bar the other night."

"I've had enough of your shit." DeShawn turned around and looked for the best path of escape—the quickest way back to the cabin, his car, and then town.

He would report Lucy at the local police station as soon as he was away from her.

He started walking, only to hear her footsteps running after him.

Lucy yanked on his shoulder; he turned to push her away. She forced a damp cloth over his mouth and nose. A sharp chemical smell shot through his nostrils to his brain.

* * *

The world was hazy and wobbled. DeShawn focused his vision, and aged wooden beams greeted him overhead. He was back in the cabin. The episode with the man had been no dream. Was he in danger?

He rolled onto his side.

Lucy was standing over him with the hammer in her hand.

DeShawn got to his feet. He held his hands out in front of him, hoping not to set her off again. "Listen, I want to get going, okay? I won't say anything."

"You still don't get it. Things are different now. It doesn't matter if you stay or go."

"Come on, Lucy. You gotta see that this isn't right. Just let me go. I don't want us to fight." DeShawn felt as though he could physically fend her off and get away without the need for any weapons. She had caught him off guard outside. He faced her prepared now, but in case, he took note of the rusty knife on a counter to his right.

"We don't have to fight. We need to kill someone." Lucy stepped toward him. "Maybe I need to knock you out again and tie you up until you understand. I like you. It would be nice to have a friend."

DeShawn had heard enough. He ran, hoping to get past her unscathed. She swung the hammer at him. It crashed into his shoulder, sending him in the direction of the counter, where he instinctively went for the knife.

Lucy was on him before he could turn around. She grabbed one of his arms. "Sinning is winning. Sinning is winning. Sinning is—"

DeShawn spun around, breaking free from her hold.

He plunged the rusty knife into her chest, just above her heart.

The knife went in a lot deeper than DeShawn expected. Lucy released him, stumbling backward, and wailing at the top of her voice. She went quiet. Her eyes widened, threatening to shoot out their sockets. She gurgled, soft, and then the sound got louder and louder.

"Fuck, what have I done?" DeShawn stared at Lucy as she tried to pull the knife out.

Green foam came out the sides of her mouth. Her body grew bigger and bigger. DeShawn had to focus to be sure, but it was true. Lucy was expanding like a balloon. Her skin became paler the more it stretched.

Something was seriously wrong, but DeShawn couldn't move.

Lucy began shaking; her body jiggled like jelly.

"What the fu—"

She exploded.

Lime-green gunk flew into the air like a science experiment gone wrong, very wrong. DeShawn ducked, but it didn't help; the slime covered him. He heard splattering all around him as Lucy's remains hit the floor. The smell was putrid.

"Holy fucking shit." He stood upright and examined the scene. The fragments of bone were a discolored brown and looked brittle. The organs and flesh were ashen gray in color. There was no blood. In its place was the green gunk, and it covered almost every inch of the cabin. He knew after seeing the guy tied up that something had been off about Lucy, but this was next-level crazy.

The knife's handle stuck out at an acute angle into the air. The blade had found home inside of something, something that wasn't green, brown, or gray. Whatever it was, it was black.

DeShawn leaned forward.

It was some type of creature. He guessed it was about five inches in length. DeShawn held his hand over his mouth as he gagged. He forced himself forward, wanting to know what it was.

He gripped the knife and wiggled it free from the creature. The creature lightened in color, changing from black to gray. Like a puff of smoke or ash in the wind, it simply dissipated into the air as if it had never existed.

DeShawn knew what it reminded him of. It had looked like a little devil, with little horns and a tiny tail.

It hadn't been red like in cartoons. Everything felt surreal, yet still made sense. Was he in shock? He recalled his mom often telling him to "watch out for them bad girls" and that they were "possessed by the Devil." If only his mom knew how true those words could be. It was unlike anything he had seen in a movie. Real life was messier. Suddenly, Lucy's infatuation with sinning added up. Sins must have been what the little devil required for sustenance.

A gentle vibration came from his pocket, pulling him from his dreamlike state. A song started playing. DeShawn exhaled, finding focus. It was his cell phone. He reached into his pocket and looked at the name. He had to answer.

"Hi, Mom," DeShawn said.

"Hey, DeShawn. Where are you? We're already setting up. You said you'd be home to give me a hand. It's Thanksgiving, remember?"

"Uh, yeah. I'll be home soon."

"Okay. One more thing—are you dressed neat?"

"Sure," he said, ignoring the putrid gunk covering him. "Why?"

"Your father is home. He decided against extending his duty."

"All right, I'm on my way."

After the call, DeShawn made his way straight home. He had chosen not to stop at the police station. No one would have believed him anyway. He didn't know if he was still in shock or if the relief of escape fueled him, but he knew he'd have to come to terms with his experience by himself. For some reason, he remained concerned about the strange egg-shaped pill Lucy had given him. He checked his eyes in the rearview mirror before climbing out of his vehicle, but his pupils looked fine. Maybe the day's events had nullified the potency of the drug—if it was even a drug. Apart from a bit of dizziness and the warmth, he had felt few effects, and there were almost no lingering symptoms.

There was a slight pain above his heart.

DARK CELEBRATIONS

THREE DEAD MEN

Maiko Hayashi stumbled to the front door of her uncle's home, using her cell phone for illumination. She had parked in the driveway, only to find an uninviting house. No lights were on, which was strange because when her uncle went out, he would leave one or two on, especially the orange light by the front door. He knew Maiko liked to come and go and had even given her a set of keys to his home.

Things got weirder as she walked by the box-shaped garage window. Using her phone to see inside, she could make out her uncle's vehicle. Maiko knocked on the front door, wondering if there had been a power failure.

"Uncle Takumo, are you home?"

Her uncle stayed on the outskirts of town. Maiko could see no lights around her, though she knew that there were houses on either side down the road leading to her uncle's place. All she could see was what little of the land the nighttime sky revealed.

Maiko knocked again. "Uncle, are you home?"

No response.

The silence screamed.

Maiko tried the front door's handle, finding it unlocked. The hairs on her forearms stood. Her concerns for her uncle compelled her into action; she pushed the door open and entered.

Maiko flicked all three switches on in the first room, the living area. These switches belonged to the orange light outside and the warm yellow lights of the living room and passageway. The scent of lavender incense tickled her nose. Nothing looked out of place in the room. It was tidy as usual. The framed photographs stood as they always had on the wall unit. All the electronics were there. The much-loved purple vase that had belonged to her deceased aunt sat on the little table next to her uncle's favorite chair.

A Japanese sword, a *katana*, safely housed in its *saya*, rested on a mount attached to the wall to her right. If Maiko's parents had a son, her uncle would have passed the sword down to him when deemed worthy. Maiko pushed the thought away. It was a thought that appeared on occasion and filled her with a hollow sadness, similar to what she felt whenever she disappointed her parents. Her uncle loved her in his own way, and she loved him.

"Uncle," she said. "Where are you?"

A clock ticking on the wall was all that replied.

Maiko made her way down the passageway. Should she call her parents and let them know she couldn't find her uncle? No—she didn't want to upset them, especially because they were busy preparing Christmas Eve dinner. It was the reason she was here, to pick her uncle up. Her parents preferred that she give him a lift to and from the house because he tended to overindulge—especially in regards to alcohol—during any festive holiday.

Maiko was home on break from college; her first semester hadn't gone as planned. Her grades were excellent, but making friends had proved difficult. As for the possible boyfriend her mother kept asking about, that didn't seem too realistic at the moment. "You just need to come out of your shell," her mother kept repeating. As if it were so easy. Seeing her uncle would make her feel better. He had a way of making her forget the difficult aspects of her life.

Relief filled Maiko when she saw his bedroom light on. She knocked on the door, which stood ajar.

"Uncle Takumo, may I come in?

Maiko entered. Her uncle wasn't in the powder-blue room. Photographs on a cabinet to her left caught her eye. Many of them were from when her family still lived in Japan. Her uncle had immigrated to America, where he served as a professor at a university, teaching ancient Japanese culture until he retired. Maiko's parents had joined her uncle in America not long after he'd left Japan. Maiko hadn't been born at that point. What she knew of her parents' homeland was what she had taken in during two visits to the country, a sum of twenty-six days spent in the land of the rising sun.

A loud *bang* caused Maiko to flinch. She turned back to the passageway, placing her hand over her heart. It beat faster than normal.

She caught her reflection in a mirror to her left. Her dark auburn hair flowed down the sides of her pale, narrow face. The concern for her uncle was evident in her strained brown eyes. Where was he? What had caused the bang? The stupidity of her internal questions made her blush. She knew exactly where he was and turned away from the mirror, not wanting to see her cheeks redden any further. The relief that her uncle was safe calmed her.

She made her way to the kitchen. The loud *bang* came again, but it didn't frighten her. It wasn't often her uncle was in such a good mood that he would be where Maiko suspected he was. In her mind she could envision him surrounded by all the items he collected, safe and happy. She wanted to skip due to her excitement, but she didn't, dismissing the idea as silliness.

Maiko slipped through the kitchen and opened the back door. Entering the night, she couldn't see much, but the shape of a building stood in the distance. It was strange that no lights shone from it if her uncle was there, but Maiko presumed he may be working in one of the back rooms. She upped her pace. The three-room structure just beyond the house was her uncle's little secret. Only Maiko and her parents knew what it was for, though her parents didn't have much interest in the place.

Another *bang* echoed.

This time it concerned Maiko. The building's door had caused the sound, and it must have slammed against the steel bin next to it. Surely that wasn't possible. There was no wind to speak of. What worried her even more was that the door now stood open.

Her uncle never left the building open, even if he was inside.

* * *

Maiko switched the light on in the first room. It was the biggest area in the building and the most impressive. She never knew where to look first. She remained mesmerized by the myriad of antiques and artifacts her uncle had amassed. Whether it was the paintings, masks, and other items hanging on the walls, or the special treasures kept in the glass cases to her right, something always fascinated her. Even the more common items on tables in the center of the room could draw her in. Maiko always saw something new. Her uncle didn't collect from one culture's past; he accumulated everything and anything of historic importance that he could get his hands on. Over the last year, he had been particularly captivated by Ancient Egypt. The books on her left caught her gaze. They filled uniquely designed bookshelves, and their pages overflowed with the history of the world. Maiko had read a few of them, though she had to read them at her uncle's place—he never allowed her to take them home.

Maiko snapped out of the room's spell. "Uncle Takumo, are you here?"

She got no response.

A hint of a cleaning product smell tickled her nose.

A bumped over table lay on the floor leading into the next room. A glass bowl had shattered alongside it. Her uncle would be furious to see the damage. She doubted he would have caused it and left it there, but then who could have done it? She considered the possibility of an intruder, but that concern ceased when she reminded herself that all the other valuables were untouched.

Maiko tiptoed into the next room and flicked on the light switch.

The illumination was bright white, which offered less warmth than the light in the first room. The room contained tools and other equipment her uncle required for repairing and cleaning his prized possessions. A large wooden workbench stood a few feet ahead of her. She inhaled the dusty, stale aroma hanging in the air, noticing tools uncharacteristically lying on the floor.

Maiko walked toward a steel door on the other side of the room. Her uncle kept the reinforced door locked—she'd tried opening it a few times when he hadn't been near. She didn't know what lay behind it. It was the only room she had never entered. Her heart beat stronger and faster as she reached toward the handle. She had been successful with two doors so far. Would the third continue the streak?

Locked.

"Uncle Takumo, are you in there?" Maiko knocked.

Shuffling came from beyond the door.

"Uncle?"

"Maiko," a raspy voice said. "Is that you?"

"Yes, Uncle." Maiko rested her ear against the door's cool surface.

"You must get out now." Her uncle banged on the door. "Run, Maiko. Run and get help."

"What? Why?" A nervous energy coursed through Maiko's veins. "I came to fetch you for dinner. Are you okay?"

"Maiko, listen to me. Something happened. I don't know how to explain it, but you must leave now. I don't know where they are."

"Do you mean burglars?" Maiko drew in a breath deeper than usual.

"No, Maiko." The handle turned, but the door didn't open. "I'm stuck in here. I lost the keys in my haste to lock behind me. I can't find them. The light doesn't work."

"Do you have a spare?"

"I do, in my bedside drawer, but it's too dangerous—"

"I'll get them," Maiko said, turning around.

"Maiko, stop," Takumo commanded. "This room has three stone tombs in it. I had three mummies in here. I won't go into the difficulties of how I obtained them, but they were my most expensive purchases. It's why I kept them hidden in this room. I'm sorry I never showed you, but ... but I didn't think this would ever happen."

"I'm confused."

"They came to life, Maiko. They rose from the dead. I know it sounds preposterous. But it happened, and they are dangerous. This is why you must run, Maiko. Get home and contact the authorities. I don't know where they are. They could return at any time. It's not safe here."

Maiko couldn't believe what her uncle was telling her. Was he playing a mean prank? That wasn't his nature at all. Had he drunken himself into a delirious stupor? That was more likely, but even in such an inebriated state, she doubted her uncle would ever believe in mummies rising from the dead. He was a pragmatic man. Plus his speech wasn't slurred.

"Uncle, I don't have time for this. I'll fetch the spare key and unlock the door. Everyone is waiting for us."

"Maiko, you're not listening to me. You're in danger, great danger—"

"No, Uncle Takumo—"

The door to the outside slammed again. Something like glass crashed onto the floor in the first room. There was somebody else entering the building. Maiko had no idea who it could be. Maybe her father had come to see what was keeping her, as she'd left her cell phone in her uncle's kitchen.

"Shut the door, Maiko!" Takumo screamed.

Maiko looked toward the entrance of the room. A tall human-shaped figure appeared before her. Dirty bandages covered its face. There were only two black holes where eyes would have been on a person.

Lowering her gaze, she saw the bandages wrapped over the figure's entire body. It held its arms out before it like a zombie in a low-budget movie. The peril took a moment to sink in, and a sheet of ice enveloped Maiko's body. A numbness had beset her. Even if she'd wanted to move, it wouldn't have mattered.

It was too late to close the door.

There was nowhere to run to.

* * *

The first time Maiko had seen the second room, where her uncle worked on items that needed attention, she was only eight years old. There were almost as many tools lying around as there were antiques and artifacts in the first room. Her uncle had warned her about touching them and scolded her when she reached for a saw lying on the edge of his workbench. As punishment, her uncle banished her from the special building for almost three years. After seeing the blood-chilling figure of the mummy, she couldn't help but wish he had never allowed her in again, no matter how beautiful the building's contents.

The mummy crossed the threshold into the room.

Maiko looked at the tools around her. No saws lay near her, but there was a sharp pointed steel instrument that looked like a large spike. She forced her body to obey her commands, overriding her current frozen status. She moved for the odd tool. In her hand, it became a weapon.

"What do you want?" Maiko asked, holding the spike out before her.

The mummy crooked its neck as it took another step toward her. Surely it couldn't hear? Even if it could, there was no way it would understand. Maiko didn't have many options and tried her luck.

"Please, just leave me alone," she said, steadying the spike in her shaking hand.

The mummy didn't answer. It continued coming for her. Its movement was slow but ominous, as if it knew there would only be one outcome. It lowered its arms, lining them up to Maiko's neck.

A strong smell of decay preceded its lunge for her.

Maiko dodged the attack. Fortunately, she had taken advantage of its slow movement, which seemed to take great effort for the intruder. It still blocked her from exiting the room, and she needed a plan. In the background, her uncle attacked the steel door and pleaded for her to escape. He even tried shouting at the mummy, hoping to attract its attention, but Maiko knew her attacker's heart beat only for her. It was a strange thought, she realized. The mummy probably did have a heart. It was usually the only organ left in the body during the mummification process. Even so, its heart hadn't pumped for many, many years.

The mummy attacked with arms outstretched.

Its fingers curled.

Maiko evaded the unwanted touch, and she plunged her weapon into the mummy's chest. She aimed where she assumed her foe's once beating organ would be. Maybe it wouldn't make a difference, but it was the best idea she had. The spike pierced the outer layer of flesh, battling to go deeper into the mummy's rough interior, which stank and looked like old beef jerky. Maiko grimaced as she forced the spike in deeper, using two hands to drive it home into the heart.

The mummy dropped its arms and took a step back. The retreat was momentary. It raised its arms again, readying for another attack. Stabbing the heart had done nothing.

Maiko ignored the perspiration running down her face and searched for another tool to turn into a weapon as the mummy came at her—its third attempt. An ax hanging on the wall caught her attention. She moved quickly and lifted it off its mount. Her undead enemy's left hand caught her hair, and it yanked down hard.

Maiko yelped, trying to break from the mummy's hold. Tears swelled in her eyes. She pulled her head forward, hoping to free herself, ignoring the pain that burned on her scalp.

The mummy released her and tried to grab her neck instead.

Maiko escaped its attempt and swung the ax in the direction of her attacker's left leg. She found a weak spot. The ax cut right through the limb, just below the knee. Dust flew out of the severed limb. The mummy buckled and fell forward. Its head bounced against the cold, hard floor. One of its gangly arms swung across the ground, knocking Maiko onto her rear.

The mummy peered up and stretched out with one of its arms as if it was going to crawl toward her. Maiko stood. She stepped back, wanting space to strike a crushing blow, but slipped on some of the dust beneath her feet. Her legs shot backward and out from under her as her arms swung forward. She held tight to the ax, which inadvertently headed in the direction of the mummy. A puff of dust, darker than that which had escaped the severed knee, ejected into the air as the ax's blade found home in her foe's skull.

The mummy stopped moving.

Its head had returned to gazing at the floor. The smell escaping its new wound took Maiko's breath away. It was a pungent stench unlike anything she had ever experienced. She also took note of the fact that it was best to aim for the head and not the heart.

"Maiko, Maiko, are you okay?" Takumo asked from behind the steel door. His voice was cracking, the concern evident.

Maiko braced through the panic that threatened to consume her. Her hands shook. "I—I'm fine. I think I killed it with the ax."

"Maiko, get out of here now. The others may return."

"All right, Uncle," Maiko said, trying to keep from bursting into tears. Fear and shock left her feeling weak. She inhaled deeply. "I'll go get help."

"Yes, yes. Get out of here, Maiko."

* * *

Maiko exited the building in a daze. The outdoors did nothing to alleviate the sudden tilt of her world. She did, however, have a moment of lucid thought. As she looked at her dirty hands, she realized she had no weapon. What if she ran into another of these monsters? She looked around for anything with which to defend herself.

She didn't want to go back into the building to find something, as that would mean seeing the grotesque mummy again. So she picked up a brick lying a few feet from her. It was the best she could find, and her car wasn't far. She sprinted away from the building, holding the brick against her chest like a professional running back protecting a football.

She slowed her pace when she could see her vehicle. Something didn't feel right, and she was thankful she had switched on the orange outside light earlier. Lowering her hand that carried the brick to her side, she stopped. Something was definitely off. Four white lights hovered behind her car. The lights were in sets of two, almost as if they were pairs of eyes. Two of them disappeared. The other two got brighter.

A shadow rounded her car.

The outside light illuminated it.

Another mummy came toward her, and she raised the brick while stepping backward. Maiko didn't know what happened to the other set of eyes, but she tried not to think about another attacker approaching from behind. She needed to focus on the one coming right at her. Her mind could only handle one monster at a time.

Turning her head, she saw that she was near the side of the house. Something—a gardening tool, perhaps—stood against the wall. She focused, trying to make out what it could be and if it would help her. She saw the handle clearly, but the rest of the object vanished into dark shadows. Maiko had no choice; she would have to wait until the right moment to use the brick and then make a break for the tool.

She kept still. It wasn't without significant effort, for unlike in the room, her mind now demanded that she bolt, flooding her with adrenaline. The mummy kept approaching. It was only a few feet from her. Maiko attempted to calm frayed nerves as her mind begged her once more to run. She didn't move. She waited, and waited. The seconds felt like an eternity.

The time to act came.

She hurled the brick at her foe.

The mummy was far too slow in moving its hands to shield itself. The brick crashed into its forehead, sending it reeling backward. A chunk of flesh fell to the ground; a puff of dust popped into the air, exiting the fresh wound. Her enemy fell to the ground.

Maiko sprinted for the tool.

She grabbed it, and relief soothed her tired limbs when she realized it was a garden fork. Its ends were sharp, as her uncle always kept his tools in good condition. She turned back to the mummy. It had found its bearings and fixated on her again. Maiko took a quick glance around the area. There was still no sign of the other pair of eyes.

She pushed through the trepidation, walking toward the mummy approaching her. Everything in her mind told her she was nuts and that she should get away, if not to her car, then anywhere. Maiko refused. The mummies moved faster in the open than she expected. She didn't want to run and have one of them find her when she was too exhausted to protect herself. Maiko had gained some confidence in stopping the first mummy. She also didn't want to leave her uncle.

Maiko waited until she was a few feet from attacker number two. She raised the fork. It was heavy, and she was getting tired. The fear and constant battle with her mind kept depleting her energy. She grimaced, commanding any strength she could find into her arms.

Maiko charged at the mummy.

She drove the fork into its face.

Her enemy had no chance preventing the gardening implement from impaling it. Maiko struck with such force that the blow knocked it backward. Maiko fell over the mummy, releasing her grip on the fork as she tumbled onto the ground, crashing hard on her back and left arm. Instinctively, she rolled over a few times to distance herself from her foe, just in case it was still after her.

She turned her head to the side, expecting another attack.

The mummy lay inert. This time, she was sure it would never rise again. The fork, apart from putting her attacker to rest, had also exposed a face that was a mixture of burned meat and hardened charcoal sludge. The adrenaline that pumped and the sight of her fallen attacker's grim visage caused a potent cocktail to shake in her core. The warm substance came up her throat.

Maiko got to her knees and wretched, splattering the ground between the mummy and her.

* * *

Maiko allowed the dizziness that rocked her after killing the second mummy to pass. She was on her back, looking at the sky. She wanted to disappear in the stars above. The night had been difficult, but it wasn't over. When she saw two stars that reminded her of the mummies' eyes she'd seen behind her car, she knew she had to get up. One of them was still around somewhere. Maiko rubbed her sore arm while she tried to ignore the pain coming from her ribs. She figured they had bruised and not broken, because she was able to breathe without too much pain while getting to her knees.

She stood.

Where is it? Where is the third one hiding? Maiko looked in the direction of her car. The mummy wasn't there. A chill embraced her exposed skin. She wasn't sure if it was because of a slight drop in the temperature or if it was something else. The sound of heavy feet dragging came from behind. She turned around.

The mummy's white eyes were less than ten feet from her.

This mummy was taller, broader than the previous two, and there was something sinister about the way its arms hung loose at its sides. The other mummies had raised their arms upon seeing Maiko and moved immediately for her. This one seemed content to stare her down. It didn't augur well.

Maiko turned back to the house and ran. The front door held her view, a tether to hope. She had left the fork behind her, but the worry was fleeting. There was a much better weapon waiting for her inside the house.

Entering the living room, she stared at the *katana*. She'd never even touched the family heirloom and doubted if even her father, Takumo's brother, had. A peculiar force held her back as she tried to step closer to the weapon. Maiko knew it was all mental. Had she a better plan, she wouldn't have chosen to use the sword. This was life or death. She would happily face her uncle's wrath once the last of the mummies had fallen.

Footsteps came from outside the front door.

The mummy entered.

Maiko took the sword off its mount. She took the *katana* out of its *saya* and turned to face her enemy. The weapon felt comfortable in her hand. A newfound confidence flooded her veins as she thought of all the possible generations of her family that may have held the weapon, some maybe even in battle as she now found herself.

The mummy rounded the coffee table and reached for her.

It was faster than the other two.

Maiko didn't flinch. She swung the *katana* once, then again; and almost as if by magic, both the mummy's arms were gone. The limbs found a resting spot on the living room floor. There was a pause in her attacker's movements. Even without arms, it came again. It lowered its head. Was it going to try and ram her like a bull?

Deciding to put it out of its misery, Maiko stepped forward and swung. The blade moved majestically through the air and decapitated the mummy with a single stroke. The head dropped to the floor, reuniting with its arms. Its body followed a moment later.

Maiko put the *katana* back in the *saya* but didn't return it to its mount. Instead, she retrieved the key for the locked room from her uncle's bedroom and made her way back to the building.

The two of them embraced as soon as they were outside.

Maiko handed the sword to her uncle. "I'm sorry for taking it, Uncle Takumo. I know I have disappointed you. I didn't know what else to do."

"No, Maiko," Takumo said, taking the sword as if it weighed twenty times its actual weight. "It is I who has disappointed you. The *katana* has always gone to the one who is most worthy in our family. And you, Maiko, are worthier than I have ever been."

Takumo got onto his knees. He held the weapon out before him. A tear ran down his aged, wrinkled cheek. "Please honor me and our family by accepting this *katana*. I should've given it to you a long time ago. I know you will always bring honor to our family."

Maiko took the sword. "Thank you, Uncle Takumo."

"I don't know how those mummies came back to life, but it may be time I get rid of some off my collection." Takumo ran his hand across his forehead. "I am lucky to have you for a niece, Maiko. Our family from generations past would be so proud. You have defeated three monsters and saved me."

Maiko bowed.

The sword had awakened something inside of her. It held so right in her hand, as if it were an extension of her body. She removed the *katana* from the *saya* and held up the blade, which shimmered under the spell of the moon. The fear from before the fight was gone. She swung the blade through the air. It glided with the same perfection as it had when striking down the mummy.

Maiko would never fear anything again.

"I doubt that telling your parents what happened would be a great idea," Takumo said, getting to his feet. "They may not believe us."

Maiko nodded.

Earlier in the day, she'd wondered what presents her parents would get her. Looking at the sword, she realized any gift from now on would pale in comparison to the one her uncle had given her. It was the gift she had earned—the gift she'd given herself.

Maiko returned the *katana* to its *saya*.

For a moment, she couldn't help but wish there were another mummy or two for her to battle.

HAPPY DARK YEAR

"Do you want me to stop the fucking car?" Cody Wheeler asked. "Because that's what I'll do. Then no one gets to go to the party."

His girlfriend, Kendall Simpson, didn't reply. She put her hand over the side of her face and leaned against the passenger-side window. The agitation boiled over within Cody. He had listened to her concerns all day, but whenever he tried to speak, she threw a fit or ignored him. He'd hoped coming back to his little hometown in California would be a time for relaxation and fun. So far, it was proving more stressful than college.

"We're only two hours from each other. I can't help that we didn't get into the same school." Cody shook his head. "I've visited you three times already. Plus, we have the holidays. We should be enjoying it."

The two-lane blacktop stretched into the night. They were on their way to a New Year's party on the outskirts of town. It was past Roy's Motel up ahead, at an abandoned barn—the perfect spot for a bash. Most people there were in their early twenties, making it the ideal place to get away with some underage drinking— the cops usually let some stuff go for New Year's, especially if the partygoers weren't causing a ruckus.

Kendall turned to him. A tear escaped one of her eyes, both of which had black makeup around them. It streaked a charcoal line over the white makeup on the rest of her face. She hummed the tune of another strange song Cody didn't know as she fixed the collar on her coat. The party required everyone to dress up. He chose to go as a Greek god, opting for a white robe and gold crown. Kendall's look unnerved him, especially considering she had long black hair and wore a peculiar red coat she kept fiddling with. There were many things Cody didn't understand about his girlfriend, and her eclectic tastes in fashion and music were only a couple of items on the list.

"What? You've got nothing else to say?" Cody asked.

"You said we could swim today. We never did."

"You realize we're in winter?"

"It's been warm the last few days."

"Are you shitting me? We didn't have time today. Kendall, you were on the swim team. You've swam just about every goddamn day of your life." Cody massaged his forehead. The two of them were athletes. Kendall, with her slim, fit body, was born a gifted swimmer, and Cody, with his muscular physique and perfect hand-eye coordination, had developed into an excellent football player.

"You didn't want to see my mother."

Cody massaged his jaw. He had been to her mother's place once. It was a beautiful two-story home overlooking the ocean. Her mother was some big-time entrepreneur with businesses and other properties scattered all over. Kendall's sister followed in her mother's footsteps, as Kendall kept reminding him. Her mother, however, had been away for some unscheduled work when they'd arrived. The two of them had spent the weekend there alone. It was where their relationship bloomed, and where the intimacy intensified. Kendall had even opened up about her past and family, except for her father. She never mentioned him much; Cody recalled only that he'd disappeared before she was born. He didn't dig any deeper, and he hadn't seen photographs of any men in her mother's home.

"We were at your mother's a while back. It's not my fault she wasn't there. I wanted to spend time with my friends for New Year's. Is that so bad? We can see your mother next week."

Kendall shook her head. "She'll be away for work next weekend."

"Is there no winning with you?"

"You didn't want my sister to come to the party."

"What? I just said we can't be babysitting her. She won't know anyone at the party." Cody cursed under his breath. He had yet to meet Kendall's sister, and a party with his friends would be the last place he'd want to entertain her family member. "You love painting me as the bad guy."

"You said we wouldn't fight anymore."

"And I don't want to. You keep on picking away. We haven't seen each other in three weeks, and now for two days straight you've gotten increasingly agitated with me."

"You promised we'd always be together."

Cody looked ahead, grinding his teeth. He had been excited for the party. It was the first time he could see his high school friends since heading off to college. He cared about Kendall, a lot, but she had a way of draining him. Maybe the two of them being two hours apart while at college would be a good thing.

Kendall rested her head against the window.

The motel was coming up. Its lights burned like a beacon of hope in the darkness. Cody could feel the earlier excitement returning. Soon he would be knocking back some beers, and Kendall's moaning would be nothing more than empty radio waves. Maybe she would even have a good time, but he doubted it.

"I really wanted to go swimming with you today," Kendall muttered.

"For fuck's sake, Kendall." Cody slapped the steering wheel, surprised how quickly the anger boiled over within him. It felt as though a volcano had exploded, spitting him out and sending him flying into a brick wall. He needed a release.

Cody turned into the parking lot of Roy's Motel.

He stopped the car.

"Get out," he said, unsure if it was a threat, or if he was being serious. He would let Kendall decide.

Kendall's face was calm. There was no sign of her usual proclivity for petulance or caustic remarks when she didn't get her way. She opened the door. Cody kept his gaze low, fearful of succumbing to her hauntingly beautiful ocean-blue eyes. He clenched his jaw shut. He needed to teach her a lesson. If they were going to be together, her unnecessary antics had to cease.

"I love you," Kendall said so softly that it was almost a whisper.

Cody didn't flinch.

Kendall climbed out of the car without uttering another word. Cody expected her to bang the door shut, but she didn't. She gently closed it behind her and took two steps away from the car, then turned around. There she stood, staring at him. He hadn't looked up, but he sensed her gaze.

Cody started the engine and drove away.

It was only when he turned back onto the road that he checked the rearview mirror. Kendall hadn't moved. Guilt tugged at him, but he ignored it. She would be fine. Everyone knew Roy, who ran the motel, and he was an okay guy. Kendall would surely ask him for a lift to the party once she accepted how immature she had acted. Either that, or she would call Cody to come back and pick her up—after she apologized, of course.

Cody turned his focus back to the road. He could at least get some alone time with his friends and maybe get a few shots down—something Kendall would have hated—before she arrived or he had to fetch her.

Kendall would be fine.

* * *

The party was already rocking when Cody arrived. Empty beer cans littered the floor, while a bunch of people dressed in all sorts of getups were dancing to his left. Tables to his right held snacks and drinks. The smell of cigarettes, sweat, and marijuana permeated the air. Cody strolled forward, keeping an eye out for his friends, but after the scene with Kendall, he decided a drink was his first objective.

Cody reached into a bucket filled with beers and ice. He grabbed one of the cans, opened it, and took a gulp. He bobbed his head to the music's beat, already feeling better. Some of the other people wore costumes that rivaled his girlfriend's in strangeness. There was someone in a werewolf costume, and a woman who wore a dirty white dress, a long black wig, and white powder over her face to make her appear like a ghost. Another dude had slicked his hair back and had those fake fangs as if he were a vampire. This was a New Year's party, not Halloween. What was wrong with people these days? Maybe Kendall wasn't that odd after all. Cody blocked the new line of thought; he was here to have fun. It had been a long year, especially as college ate most of his free time.

He decided it was time to locate his friends.

A girl walked by him, headed toward one of the tables.

She wore a body-hugging black dress that showed off her stunning physique. If that weren't enough to draw eyes, she also wore wings made of blue feathers, and her hair was white with blue highlights. Her hips swayed ever so slightly as she walked. Cody forgot about his friends. He turned, watching her. For some reason, she stuck out. She was unlike anyone here. In fact, she was unlike anyone he had ever seen.

Cody turned to a table nearby, finding rows of colorful shots lined up on its surface. It was the liquid courage he needed. He lifted a green-colored shot and downed it. It was a lot sweeter than he had expected. Still, the nerves retreated as if alcohol were some magic elixir, or was it merely a mental thing? It worked, which was what mattered.

He targeted a red-colored one.

"Wait," a female voice said.

Cody turned. Her appearance caught him off guard at first. She had a white bandage wrapped around her face, like the mummies he'd seen in horror films. There were holes cut out for her eyes and mouth. He wanted to laugh at how strange some of the people got with their costumes, but he restrained himself and dropped his gaze. His amusement vanished as he found himself staring in awe at her beautiful body. It wasn't the body of the young women he usually saw. Hers was more mature and curvier—the body of a *real* woman, as some of his friends would say.

"You drink at that pace, you may not make the New Year," the woman said. Her mature age was now evident in her confident, unwavering voice.

"I'll be fine," Cody said. "I'm just looking for a little boost to start the night."

"Oh, I see." The woman reached over the table. "You should try this one, then."

Cody took the blue shot she handed him and dumped it down his throat as she made her way around him. "Thanks. What's your—"

He turned to find the woman gone; she'd disappeared into the crowd of people headed to the dance floor. The shot had been more potent than the first, and Cody grimaced because the aftertaste left a harsh bitterness in his mouth. He couldn't see the woman in the ever-changing crowd, but his disappointment didn't last long. The girl with the blue highlights was still at one of the tables. She waved when she caught his stare.

"Excellent," Cody whispered, making his way to the mysterious girl, a puzzle he wanted to solve.

"Hey there, I'm Cody," he said, offering his hand.

The girl shook it. "I'm Hannah. It's nice to meet you."

"Nicer to meet you, Hannah." Cody scanned the table for a beer. "Are you from around here? I don't recognize you."

"Nope, I'm from out of town."

Cody found a light beer. It would have to do.

"This party is kind of boring," Hannah said.

"I see." Cody took a sip from the beer. "What do you find *not* boring then?"

"Hmm, there are a lot of things. I feel like doing one thing in particular though."

"Yeah, what do you have in mind? Maybe I can help."

Hannah looked at him, her pale blue eyes mesmerizing. "I want to go swimming."

"What is it with you women and swimming?" Cody said, while repressing the thought that he had a girlfriend.

"What do you mean?"

"Umm, nothing."

"I can assure you, Cody, swimming with me tonight would be unlike any experience with any other woman."

"How so?" Cody sipped his beer.

"For starters, I didn't pack my bikini."

Cody resisted the urge to spit out his mouthful of beer. His eyes watered as a result, but it was better than spraying Hannah. He righted himself, like when he mentally focused for the second half of a game when his team was behind on the scoreboard. The inner desire to succeed quickly rekindled his ego.

"Well, Hannah. You've found the right man. I know the perfect place."

Hannah smiled.

* * *

Cody took Hannah to a secluded area on the banks of the local lake, a spot which was only a ten-minute drive from the party. He and Kendall had often come here to hang out and swim. In fact, he figured it was probably Kendall's favorite place. They'd even had their first date here, and a couple more since. He cursed himself internally for thinking about Kendall.

The place was scenic, with tall trees surrounding this section of the lake and the nighttime sky shining over the calm water's surface. Hannah couldn't contain her grin as she admired the spot. Cody could barely hide his, but for other reasons. Hannah strolled nearer to the water. She took off her shoes and placed them next to her large blue handbag.

"You know," Cody said, "one of the rivers connected to the lake makes its way to the ocean."

"I know," Hannah said. She proceeded to remove her clothes.

Cody inhaled deeply.

"Come on, Cody." She winked at him. "Don't be shy."

A strange thought popped up in the fore of his mind. He wondered if he should check his phone, which he had left in his car. A peculiar sound gliding through the air attracted his attention instead. It took him a second to realize Hannah was humming a song.

She stopped. "You coming?"

"Yes."

Cody marched toward her, taking his shirt off. He paused to watch her remove her bra, admiring her perfectly shaped breasts, and then clumsily unbuckled his belt and dropped his pants. When he looked again, Hannah was naked from head to toe. She stared at the lake, transfixed, as if under a spell.

"Aww, shit," Cody said, standing in his underwear. "I could get a blanket from the car—I think there's one in the trunk—but I don't have a condom on me."

"I don't care about that," Hannah said, continuing to face the body of water ahead of her. "Plus, we're going in."

"Awesome."

The temperature was mild, but the water would be cool in winter. It didn't matter. Nothing would stop him.

"But before we do, I want to show you something."

"Okay." Cody was unsure what else she could show him. She turned and walked toward him with the moonlight illuminating her stunning shape. "Umm..."

"Shhh." Hannah placed her index finger over Cody's lips. "Do you hear that?"

"Hear what? I don't hear anything."

"Our guest has arrived."

"What guest?"

"I'd better get dressed." Hannah smiled. "But first, Cody, look at this."

She pressed her palms together as if in prayer and pointed her fingers at Cody, moving her hands closer to his face. Confusion filled him. Was she joking about a guest coming? He hoped she was teasing about putting her clothes back on. Her fingers were right in front of his face. She blew between her hands, and a sparkling blue dust burst out from between her fingers.

The dust spread over Cody's face, mimicking how water flowed rather than how particles of dust would normally flutter aimlessly through the air.

He couldn't help but inhale, expecting a sweet aroma to tickle his sense of smell, but reality was harsh. The dust had a foul stink, like the stench of fish when you walked near the docks after the fishermen had a successful day at sea.

"What the hell?"

"Sit." Hannah winked at him.

"There's no way I'm sitting. What was that?"

"Sit down." Her voice was less playful now; her words were a command.

Cody's legs bent, sending his rear onto the ground.

He sat, but he hadn't wanted to. His arms folded, and his gaze turned to the lake. Something was wrong. He wasn't directing the movements of his body, and he could sense all control slipping away.

"You're allowed to breathe," Hannah said.

His senses dulled. He was losing the ability to comprehend his situation with every passing second.

"I want you to lie down and close your eyes," Hannah said.

Cody felt the hard ground beneath his back. Time became immeasurable. The world went dark.

* * *

"Did I not tell you they're all the same?"

"Yes, you did. But—but he was special. He was nice to me. I love him."

Cody, on his back, couldn't move, but he could hear. He didn't know how long he had been in the near-catatonic state, but he was slowly regaining some of his senses. In his head, he replayed the two voices he'd heard; they were both female. He knew the speakers, but their names were just out of reach. Cody wanted to turn and see who the voices belonged to. Had he been in total control of his mind, he would've known their names in a second.

"It feels like that with any man for us."

"I'm sad he left with you."

Cody recognized the latter voice. It was Kendall's.

"You haven't been in the water for a while. You're losing some of your potency. That's why he was pulling away from you. He was reverting to his natural self. Men are all animals at heart. You knew this would happen if you didn't keep the hold strong. Mother always says, 'Behind every good man is a strong woman controlling him.'"

"I thought he loved me for me," Kendall said. "I thought he would love me without the hold."

"I'm sorry, little sister. It doesn't work that way for us. It's both our blessing and our curse. We can control them, but they'll never truly love us. You'll become accustomed to it in time. The first one is always hard."

Kendall sighed. "I guess you're right, Hannah."

Cody flinched. Hannah. That's who the other voice belonged to. The seriousness of his situation was clear. He had to claim ascendancy of his own mind. He needed to convince Kendall he'd made a mistake. She would forgive him. She had forgiven him when he'd hurt her in the past.

"Mother is here," Hannah said. "She was getting worried about you."

"Really?" Kendall asked. "Where is she?"

"We came together. She's still at the party. You know she doesn't get much time to have fun."

Cody tried to move his right leg. He wanted it to kick. The attempt didn't quite work, but through the effort, he was able to get his foot to twitch. It wasn't enough, and he focused. Like a brick shattering a window, all movement returned without warning as he lifted his leg up and slammed it down. His heel banged against the ground, sending a jarring pain up his calf. Had he alerted both girls to his awakening? He turned to his side, searching the area their voices had come from.

Kendall and Hannah stood a few feet from him, watching. Hannah was fully clothed, minus the wings. Cody realized he was still in his underwear.

"Kendall," he said, "I can explain."

Kendall turned around, choosing to face the lake instead of him.

Cody stumbled to his feet, but as he took a step to his girlfriend, Hannah came between them. She placed her hands together as she had when she'd blown the strange dust onto his face.

"Oh, fuck no you don't." Cody slapped her hands. The dust flew harmlessly to her side. She didn't seem concerned.

Cody pushed past her.

He caught her taking a step toward him in his peripheral vision; she raised her right arm. Cody turned, hoping to get his arms up to defend himself. She whistled, a haunting yet mellifluous tune that sounded as if it came from everywhere at once.

The world appeared distorted, as if he were in a bubble.

His mind shut down; his body followed.

* * *

The moon shone bright in the night sky. Cody's head beat with pain, and he remembered Hannah whistling but couldn't recall the tune. He tried to focus. The night had taken a bad turn, and he feared delirium would set in. He was on his back, which he knew easily with the sky directly above, but the surface beneath him was cold and soft, like liquid. That wasn't possible, was it?

He turned his neck. Hannah's head was sticking out of the surface of the lake. Cody couldn't find the land beyond her.

"Other side, genius," she said.

Cody turned the other way. Kendall looked back at him. She was also in the water. The two women were holding him up on the surface of the lake. The confusion of how they managed to stay perfectly afloat came to the fore, but he pushed it aside. He had other concerns. Tears streaked Kendall's face. There were chains around his wrists and legs.

"What the fuck is this?" he asked, trying to turn over.

It was no use. The two girls gripped him tight.

Their strength was undefeatable.

"Hey, let me go. What the hell?"

"I told her to do it before you came to," Hannah said, "but she wanted to say goodbye."

Cody looked to his girlfriend. "Kendall. What's going on?"

"I am so sorry, Cody. It must be this way now. I lost my hold on you. We can't risk you knowing. Maybe if you had brought us to the water more often, this wouldn't have happened. Nevertheless, please know you were special to me."

"Please, please, Kendall," Cody said. Tears formed in his eyes, but he didn't care. He wanted to be back on the land, safe again. "I love you, Kendall. You have to believe me."

"I'm sorry, Cody. That's just my hold on you. You feel it again because I'm in the water, and my power grows strong once more. This is the way it is. You were the first man I learned to control, and I really did love you, even if you didn't love me. I thought we could be together forever."

"For fuck's sake, just listen to me—"

"Bye, Cody. Know that this is an honor."

"Fuck, wait—"

The two women dove below the surface, pulling Cody with them. He tried to take as deep a breath as possible. The panic crawled throughout his limbs like a million tiny newborn spiders.

Down to the bottom of the lake they went. Kendall and Hannah swam away from him, but as Cody tried to return to the surface, he realized what the chains were for. The women pulled them tightly around him so he couldn't escape. His vision blurred, and Kendall and Hannah seemed to move with inhuman speed.

When they locked the chains to a large weight on the bottom of the lake, Cody got a clear view of the two women. Everything looked normal about Hannah's and Kendall's upper bodies, and then his gaze found their waists. From there, they resembled sea creatures more than humans. They had tails like fish. It wasn't an illusion, no matter how hard Cody tried to convince himself he'd never awoken after his last passing out.

This was happening.

The burning in his lungs as he struggled for air confirmed his reality.

He was going to drown, murdered by two mermaids. His girlfriend, who he had known throughout high school, was a fucking mermaid. *Mermaid.* The word echoed in his mind. He thought of all the TV shows he had seen featuring them. Weren't they meant to be peaceful and helpful?

Cody could hear Kendall humming one of her strange songs. The water amplified the sound. He glanced at her as she floated before him, but he refused to make eye contact. He didn't care if her visage was one of sadness. He didn't deserve this.

He looked toward the surface, hoping someone or something would save him. Bright colors exploded above. *Fireworks.*

The New Year had arrived.

Cody needed to breathe, and he accidentally swallowed a mouthful of water. He coughed, expelling any air in his lungs.

He looked for Kendall.

A massive dark cloud had replaced her. It stretched across his entire view. It appeared to have some form—a sea creature with human parts, but different from the mermaids—as if it was a type of hybrid monster. Cody couldn't believe it. The sheer magnitude of what he saw caused him to forget about his burning lungs.

"Father," he heard Kendall say, "I have my first sacrifice for you."

DYING VALENTINE

Daniel Hill's musky cologne permeated the interior of his car. He had doubled his usual amount when applying the fragrance. He needed to look, feel, and smell on point tonight. Perspiration building under his arms, on his shoulder blades, and over the middle of his chest threatened to thwart his plan. No victory came against the sweat when he was nervous. The cool night couldn't even aid him. The reassuring text he'd received from his girlfriend, Julia, had also failed to calm the swelling nerves within. He applied more pressure to the accelerator, hoping the increase in speed would shift his focus away from the wave of emotion before it turned tidal.

It was Valentine's Day, and the romantic plans he'd been tinkering with derailed two days ago, when Julia informed him her parents invited him to dinner for the first time. He couldn't understand why they picked Valentine's Day, of all days, to do the whole meet and greet. He'd been with her for six months; there had been many opportunities to invite him around. Every time he dropped Julia off or picked her up, she either ushered him away or was eager to get going. Daniel didn't even know what they looked like, and it didn't help that his mind kept projecting Julia's father as a tall, muscular man eager to protect his daughter from the cold, cruel world at all costs. All Julia had said was that they were nice and would like him. At least she didn't have siblings. No giant brother to go with the giant father was always a bonus.

After dinner, Daniel had plans to take Julia to a movie. She loved to make out in the dark of the cinema. So, there was some reward if he could get through the first part of the evening. Plus, she would be sleeping over at his place tonight. That always meant good things.

Daniel glanced at the seat next to him. It was empty. That wasn't right, and he racked his brain, trying to think of what was off about the lingering image.

"Shit," he said, slamming on the brakes.

He made an illegal U-turn.

Daniel had forgotten his wallet, as well as the chocolates and roses he'd bought for Julia. There was no way he was going to rock up to her place empty-handed. The clock ticking on the dashboard was against him. He found the accelerator to be his friend again.

He tried his best to push for time where he could. Luckily, most of the roads back to his place were quiet. Turning into his residential area, he tried to remember where he had last seen his wallet, the chocolates, and the roses. His hopes to cut down on time were forlorn because he couldn't recall if he'd left them in his bedroom, on the kitchen counter, or on the little table by the front door.

He hoped it was the latter.

Taking the last turn to his place, he checked the time on the dash, calculating he would be at least twenty minutes late. His sweating had also gotten worse; the stickiness spread all over. This caused itching to break out over random areas of his body. A warm feeling, like an invisible noose, tightened around his neck. He looked up, shaking his head as he caught his reflection in the rearview mirror. His short black hair, which he'd neatly styled before leaving home, had reverted to its usual messy morning look.

"This is bullshit," he said, looking to the road.

A strange figure dressed in white was crossing ahead of him. At first Daniel thought it was all part of his imagination, or an illusion created by the shadows of the night, but as his vehicle's lights illuminated the figure, he knew she was real, very real. The world went cold, and all of his previous concerns fell away as one fear hardened like frigid ice in the center of his mind.

He was going to hit the person.

He slammed on the brakes and bashed the horn.

It was too late. All his actions did was cause the person to freeze up and look at him, revealing the shocked visage of a young woman. It was the last thing he saw before the impact. The black hair that cascaded down to her shoulders, the bright pink lips, and the eyes widened in fear stained the fore of his mind.

The *thud* of the car knocking her body rattled Daniel's brain.

The woman flew into the air. Her white dress flapped at her sides, reminding Daniel of a strong gust of wind yanking a sheet from a clothesline. The flailing body seemed graceful in the air, as if it were all part of some stage show. There was nothing graceful about her descent back to earth. She met the ground hard, and then skidded until she came to a stop.

"Please get up," Daniel muttered. "Please, please, get up."

The woman didn't move.

* * *

Daniel left his car in the middle of the road with the driver's door standing open. His headlights shone over the woman. He ran to her, pleading with every deity he could recall that she wasn't dead. She remained inert. Nothing about her unnatural body position—arms crooked above her head and legs folded behind her back—reassured him that his life wasn't going to take a much different route than he had envisioned. It was amazing how quickly his mind attacked with images of a jail cell, Julia with another guy, and his mother in tears. He had only wanted to fetch his wallet and the chocolates and roses he'd forgotten. It didn't seem a fair price to pay. Maybe if he had been more of an asshole, he wouldn't get into these situations.

He kneeled before the woman. "Miss, are you okay?"

He felt her wrist, which was warm, hoping for a pulse while surveying the rest of her body. Her long, matted black hair covered most of her face. Daniel had the urge to move the hair away, so he could see her eyes, but he didn't. He feared seeing a lifeless stare. There were no visible injuries except for a crimson tear running from a minor cut on her calf.

There was a heartbeat.

"Hey, are you okay?" Daniel asked, resisting the impulse to shake her. "Please, please, be okay."

"Let go of me," a soft female voice muttered.

Daniel moved his head back. Was he was hearing things? There was no wind to play tricks on his mind. The night, unlike his insides, was calm. Was the voice really coming from the woman on the ground? He wanted to look around, but he couldn't take his eyes off of her.

"Are you talking?" Daniel spoke the first thought that came to mind.

"Yes," the woman said, turning her face. "Let go of my wrist."

Daniel dropped his gaze. He'd yet to release her wrist after checking her pulse. In fact, his grip had tightened. "I'm sorry," he said, letting go.

She turned onto her stomach, placing shaking arms before her, trying to push herself up.

"Here," he said, "let me help you."

"You've done enough. Now back the fuck up."

Daniel obeyed reluctantly. He retreated with his arms still ahead of him, ready in case she fell.

She grimaced as she got to her knees. Inhaling deeply, she attempted to stand. Apart from a brief wobble when she tried to correct her crooked stance, she seemed to be doing okay.

"Do you want me to take you to a hospital?" Daniel asked.

The woman looked at him, moving her hair away from her eyes. "Hundred dollars."

"What?"

"Are you deaf?" she asked, surveying the quiet neighborhood. "One hundred dollars and I won't report that you hit me. Unless you want to go to jail?"

Daniel considered his options. She had been in the middle of the road. Had he really done anything wrong? Was he speeding at the time? He couldn't recall. She seemed fine now, and a part of him wanted to alert the traffic authorities to the accident. Wasn't that correct procedure? Something about paying her off didn't feel right. His new predicament bypassed the shock of the accident; Daniel conceded and decided. There was no need to take any risks if she was so eager to move on from the incident. He reached toward his pants pocket. "Shit, I left my wallet at my house."

"That's bullshit."

"No, really. I was on my way back home to get it."

"Well, then," she said, patting some dust off of her chest. "I guess we're going to your place. I could use a little cleanup anyway. You don't mind, do you? I mean, you did almost kill me."

"Um," Daniel said, buying time. No alternatives came to the fore of his mind. "Yes, that sounds fine."

"Good."

Who was this girl? Daniel couldn't figure her out. She didn't fear climbing into a vehicle with a stranger—a stranger who had moments ago hit her with his car. Now she was going with him to his place. Time wasn't his friend, and he shelved such concerns for the moment. He needed an excuse to explain why he was so late when Julia asked him. Car trouble? Perfect. Women always fell for that, didn't they?

He climbed into his car, started it up, and unlocked the passenger door.

The mysterious woman climbed in.

He had to play it cool. Give her the money she wanted and get back over to Julia as soon as possible.

Surely it would all be plain sailing from here.

* * *

Daniel led Lilly into his living room. He had learned her name during the drive, but he wasn't sure if it was even a real name. She didn't look like a Lilly. What he did know was that he needed to proceed with haste. Julia and her family were waiting. At least the unexpected turn of the night had vanquished his earlier nerves. Meeting Julia's parents no longer seemed a moment of doom and despair.

Lilly walked to the center of the room, barely even glancing around. She lifted her dress up.

"Oh," Daniel said, "let me show you where the bathroom is."

Lilly didn't stop. She pulled her dress over her shoulders and dropped it to the floor.

It hit Daniel hard, like taking a baseball to the jaw: all she wore underneath her dress was a red G-string. Her toned, shapely, body personified beauty and perfection. Whomever she had been going to see on Valentine's was missing one incredible gift. He ceased such thoughts, but it was hard. Lilly had turned around, and he couldn't help but notice her perky breasts. Both pink nipples had piercings. A colorful tattoo of a unicorn flying over a rainbow covered her abdomen. A tattoo of a purple bear holding a book rested on her right shoulder. Her belly button was pierced, and—

"Are you okay?" Lilly asked.

"Yeah," Daniel said, looking up. Her body was like a colorful canvas that he wanted to continue to explore. Julia didn't have tattoos, and had only pierced her ears. *Pull yourself together*, he told himself. This wasn't the time to lose focus.

"You're more shaken from the accident than me." Lilly bent down to examine the cut on her leg.

"I have a girlfriend. I love her."

Lilly chuckled. She stood straight again. "Where's your bathroom, Prince Charming?"

"Over there. Let me show you." Daniel walked past her.

He paused by the kitchen counter. The chocolates, the roses, and his wallet all sat on the granite top. He grabbed the wallet.

"Here's your money." He took out the only bill he had. Even though he always used his card, he always kept a hundred—in case of an emergency. Like the pack of condoms he'd kept in his wallet since he began dating Julia, he never needed the cash before tonight. Julia had told him they didn't need condoms when having sex. She didn't want anything between them; she knew he was the one for her. Daniel, taken aback by her words then, now reciprocated her feelings. The condoms he should have chucked away long ago. He was glad he kept the money idea going, though.

Lilly tucked the bill into her G-string. "The bathroom?"

"It's this wa—"

Loud banging on the front door rattled the windows in the living room.

Daniel turned away from Lilly. Who it could be? Chad, one of his good friends, was the most likely candidate. He liked to come over unannounced and get a break from his girlfriend. That wasn't a problem as long as Daniel could get rid of him before he saw Lilly. He made his way to the front door but stopped about three steps from it.

"One second," Daniel said to the door.

He turned to Lilly and whispered, "Put on your clothes and stay out of view."

Lilly shook her head.

"Please."

Another knock made him turn back to the door. Internally, he tried to return to his usual easygoing demeanor so as not to alert Chad to anything suspicious once he opened for his friend. Daniel reached for the handle, but paused. He'd specifically told Chad he would be out tonight, and Chad had told him he was taking his girlfriend out as well. It couldn't be Chad, but then who?

"Open the door, Daniel," Julia said. "You're late. Why didn't you answer your phone? I called you three times."

Daniel looked back at Lilly. She shrugged, smiling. She knew his position but continued to stand there in her G-string.

"Daniel, open the damn door," Julia said, knocking again.

"Please," Daniel whispered to Lilly.

She held her hand out, rubbing her index finger and thumb together. "Another hundred," she whispered.

Daniel nodded. He knew he would have to go and withdraw it, but right now he needed to focus on one problem at a time. His mind raced, searching for ways to get out of this mess. How would he explain the woman in his house? Bending the truth slightly seemed his only way forward. He definitely couldn't mention giving Lilly money. Lilly put on her dress and took a seat on the sofa. That was at least one problem taken care of.

Daniel opened the front door.

Julia entered. Her blonde locks flowed down to her pale pink sweater. Her makeup accentuated her blue eyes and full lips. She smiled at Daniel. It was a smile that always seemed to activate a flurry of butterflies in his core. Yes, it was cheesy to feel this way, but that was the effect she had on him. No other girl before her could captivate him as she did.

"Hey, babe," Daniel said. "I—uh, need to—"

"Who is this?" Julia asked, staring at Lilly.

Lilly stood and smiled in return.

"I bumped her with my car. I brought her here, so she could clean up."

"Hi," Lilly said, walking toward Julia.

Julia looked her over. When she focused on the cut on the woman's leg, she stepped forward. "Oh my," she said, shaking Lilly's hand. "Are you okay?"

"Yes, I'm fine. It was just a little bump. I was so silly to be crossing at such a bad part of the road. It was my fault, really. Your boyfriend was kind enough to invite me to fix myself up. I've got big plans tonight," she said, winking, "it being Valentine's Day and all."

Daniel, fearful any more words could make Julia suspicious, stepped forward. "I was about to show Lilly where the bathroom was." He gestured for Lilly to follow him.

Lilly complied.

When Daniel returned, he took a seat on one of the living room sofas.

"I don't like her. She's weird." Julia frowned as she sat alongside Daniel. She placed the overnight backpack she had brought with her on the coffee table.

Daniel couldn't believe his luck. There had been no tantrum from Julia when she walked in. Lilly had also acted as smooth as the two hundred dollars she would cost. Overall, despite the money lost, he'd dodged some bullets.

"She'll be gone soon." He rested his hand on Julia's thigh.

"She's still weird," Julia said. "Did you see the tattoo on her shoulder?"

"Not really."

Julia sighed.

The sound triggered an alarm within him: the rest of the money. The last thing Daniel needed was to have Lilly throw a fit over not getting paid. Even if she didn't resort to such a scene, he couldn't risk her doing anything to destabilize the situation. He needed an excuse to leave. "I'm going to the pharmacy real quick."

"What for?"

"I want to get her some strong pain pills and maybe some disinfectant and other stuff. I can't let her go like that."

He expected a protest, but it didn't come. Instead, Julia bit her bottom lip as if she was deep in thought.

"Do you want me to go instead? You're already shaken up."

"No." He tried to smile reassuringly. "I'll be okay."

"Fine. McCarthy's pharmacy will be open, but that'll be at least a twenty-minute drive."

"I'll be quick."

Julia frowned.

"I mean careful."

He leaned forward and kissed her on the cheek.

* * *

Daniel didn't get too far. He had exited their neighborhood when he remembered he didn't have his wallet. It sat on the counter again after he gave Lilly the initial hundred dollars. He turned around and made his way home, where he parked the car on the side of the road.

He climbed out of the vehicle, scanning the neighborhood. There was no activity, and it was as quiet as when he left. That was a good sign. It meant Julia and Lilly hadn't suddenly decided to have a go at each other.

Entering his home, he didn't see Julia. She must have gone to help Lilly. This seemed too good to be true; he could sneak in and out before anyone noticed. The only negative was that he feared Lilly might spill the beans about the money, but he told himself not to worry. She had done so well since Julia arrived. Why would she throw it all away now?

A high-pitched scream turned his blood to ice.

He rushed to the bathroom and opened the door.

A potent stench hit him. It was a combination of metal and vomit. The first thing he saw was blood splattered all over the floor, on the bath, and even on some of the walls. The scene resembled something from the horror movies that Julia didn't enjoy watching with him. Lilly lay with her head over the bathtub. Her arms were also inside the tub, but her legs remained spread across the floor. All she wore was the red G-string. A figure stood to his left near the sink, but it wasn't Julia.

It was an old woman wearing a red cloak. Her hair was white and thin. There were more than a few bald patches, revealing pinkish skin. Her cracked lips were a light purple, while her eyes were almost gray.

"Who the fuck are you?" Daniel asked.

"Damn it. Why did you come back so soon, Daniel? I was just going to take a dip and then clean up to make it look like a suicide."

The old woman sounded exactly like Julia, except . . . she was probably in her eighties, nineties even. Daniel stepped back. His foot slipped on some of the blood on the tiled floor. He corrected himself, managing to keep from falling to the ground.

"I don't understand." He held his hands up before him like mini shields and took another step back. "Is she okay?" he asked, looking at Lilly.

"No, she's dead. I can't explain everything right now, but I will," the old woman said. "I need to sort out some things before you do something stupid."

"Who the fuck are you? What have you fucking done?" Daniel shouted. His blood boiled, and he feared for Julia's safety, while remaining perplexed by the old woman's voice. He reached for her throat.

His arm stopped halfway to its target. He couldn't move it. It was as if an invisible wall of concrete had encased it. He tried flexing his fingers, but like the rest of his limb, they refused to move.

The old woman sighed. "Oh, Daniel. Things could've been so different. Why did you have to come back so soon? I only needed a few more minutes."

"I—"

His mouth closed. He hadn't wanted it to, but like his arms, it was now no longer under his control.

"Shhh," the old woman said. "I need you to do a few things for me. Nod if you understand."

There was no way Daniel would nod, except he noticed his view kept rocking up and down. He was nodding.

"Good. I want you to move her away. I need a quick dip to store some power for the rest of the night."

Daniel could sense himself moving forward, and he witnessed his arms lifting Lilly up. No longer in control of any part of his being, he was nothing more than a marionette playing to his new master's whims. He watched himself dump Lilly on the bathroom floor, alongside the bath.

"Perfect." The old woman climbed into the tub but remained standing. She took off the red cloak, revealing the side of her naked body. She tossed the cloak next to Julia's backpack on the bathroom counter.

She faced Daniel.

Her body dominated Daniel's view. Her wrinkled skin had faded like an old newspaper. Spots of discoloration, maybe even decay, invaded everywhere he could see. Green puss escaped from some of the cracks in her skin. Her breasts, pale with shades of blue, hung below her waist. She wasn't just old. She was ancient—closer to nine hundred than ninety. If a person could have lived that long, Daniel figured this was what they would have looked like. If Daniel could have retched, he'd have done so in buckets.

"Not bad for three hundred, eh?" the old woman said, winking.

Daniel couldn't reply.

"I know it sucks to see me as I am." The old woman pouted, faking a sad face. "Unfortunately, it has to be this way whenever I'm in the restoration process. In a few minutes, I'll look just as you remember me."

She bent down and sat in Lilly's blood.

Grabbing a sponge from the side of the bath, she started humming as she bathed in the copper-smelling crimson fluid. The tune was a popular song, always on the radio. Daniel knew someone who loved the song. In fact, it was their favorite song.

It was then, the realization like someone stabbing Daniel's brain with an icicle, that he finally accepted the truth: this old woman was Julia.

* * *

After her bathing session, Daniel watched Julia pull the plug. When most of blood had drained, she climbed out and commanded him to strip and stand in the bath with his arms behind his back. Her time in the tub had worked wonders. The cracks in her face were already clearing up. Her skin was getting some color back, and even her breasts began to win the war against gravity.

"I'm a witch, Daniel." She reached into the tub to put the plug back in. "I understand that's hard to hear, but you deserve the truth. I know killing an innocent girl and then bathing in her blood may seem a little weird. But it's about survival. Like anyone else, I don't want to die. I wish you could've understood, but when I saw your face, when you looked at me after entering the bathroom, I knew it would never be."

She searched inside the backpack she had brought, and then removed a blade stained with blood. "I was going to lie to you about my parents again tonight, make up some excuse that they were out. They died a long, long time ago. I was also going to cast the spell tonight to make you start falling out of love with me—after we made love once more. It would've taken a few months for the effect to be completely gone. I didn't want to ever hurt you. You just *had* to come back and catch me, though. I couldn't resist after seeing that innocent girl. You had to put the temptation before me. I can't always control myself. I knew it would bring some attention, a girl committing suicide in your home. But, over the many years, I've gotten away with these things many times. I felt sure I would again. Unfortunately for you, and contrary to what you might believe, there is no spell to make you forget what you saw."

She leaned forward and kissed him on the cheek.

"Happy Valentine's Day," she whispered.

Tingling warmth came from her touch, and a current seemed to enter his pores where her lips graced his skin. A heat lingered over the spot when she pulled away. Was this a spell of some kind? For some reason her evermore-youthful appearance wasn't as troubling, and Daniel could sense his feelings for her swirling in his stomach again.

"I don't want you to suffer, so I'll do this quickly. Take another step back in the bath for me. Oh, be careful not to slip—there's still some blood."

Julia smiled as she held the blade up, reminding Daniel of an athlete about to launch a javelin. It felt wrong, very wrong. Daniel couldn't even beg for mercy. He realized why Julia stood in such a funny pose and why she held the blade the way she did.

She was going to stab him in the face.

"You know what? I can't do this." Julia lowered her hand. "You were so nice to me. I remember all the kisses and the touches. I haven't felt such love in decades."

Something tugged at Daniel's mind. It was weak, but it was there. Hope. If he could just talk, he could tell Julia he would never mention her being a witch to anyone. *Talk, talk, talk*, he told himself. No matter how hard he focused, nothing came out. After all they had been through in the last six months, he couldn't believe she'd end it like this. He remembered the first time they met and how he had slammed a door into his hand; she'd kicked at the door, then turned to him and promised she'd always be there for him. It had been an unusual thing to say to someone you'd just met, but he'd come to learn nothing was the usual with Julia.

"You want to talk, don't you?"

Daniel wanted to scream "Yes!" but he couldn't. He couldn't even nod. He remembered the time they ate pizza outside, staring at the starry sky above while telling each other their dreams for the future.

"I have an idea," Julia said. "Reach out with your arm."

Daniel's hand entered his view. He remembered the time he burned it trying to cook her dinner. She had responded by kissing every conceivable spot on it.

Julia placed the blade into his hand. "This will make it easier for both of us. When I say 'Now,' I want you to stab yourself in the face. It's best this way, as I don't want to waste too much blood to kill you. I will cut the proper arteries to bathe in your blood after you're dead."

Daniel couldn't plead for his life. He couldn't even shake his head, but he knew his hand had tightened around the blade. This couldn't be happening, even if she was a witch. They had spent too many intimate moments together. He remembered the time they stood on his bed after making love and danced, holding each other as they swayed to a symphony of silence.

Julia stepped back. She had almost returned to looking like the young and beautiful girl he knew.

There was no way she would do it. Maybe she only wanted to scare him a bit, to make sure he'd never tell.

He remembered the time they had gone to the local park for a picnic, only for the rain to come down. It had been then when she first told him that she loved—
"Now."

SPRING OUTBREAK

There are breakups that end fast. They're a razor blade to the wrist. The cut is clean, and as soon as enough blood taps out, memories fade, feelings vacate, and pain subsides. There are breakups that take forever to die. They feel as if the Devil's minions have dragged you over the hot coals, sharp thorns, and jagged rocks of hell's floor, only for you to discover you've reached the waiting area.

Gwen Montgomery had come to know the latter.

"I wonder what he's doing now," she said, placing her book on the sand next to her. They had been at the beach for nearly an hour, and she'd failed to get past page two. The sun sat high in the pellucid sky. There were no clouds to draw her attention away from the gnawing thoughts plaguing her mind.

"The whole point of coming to Mexico was so you could get away from all that," her friend from college, Haley Miguel, said. "I don't want you to fight to keep an asshole like you did the last few months. You deserve better. Anyway, think of all the fun we're going to have when we meet back up with the rest of the girls tonight."

A breeze caressed Gwen's neck. It moved upward and kissed her cheeks, cooling her warm skin. She inhaled deeply while listening to the activity of the beach. The salty air did nothing to clear her mind. She ran her hand over her towel and onto the sand, feeling the grains shift between her fingers. The texture reminded her of the sandpit her grandfather had dug for her and her brother, Thomas, when they were kids. Everything had been an adventure, and outlooks were always positive back then. All that changed when her brother passed away from leukemia at age fourteen. Gwen had been sixteen. The three years since were anything but an adventure, and finding positives seemed more elusive than finding alien life. She missed Thomas more than she missed her ex-boyfriend, Ralph. Although being with her ex had allowed her to bury some of the crushing feelings of loss for Thomas, now the sadness returned, and it overwhelmed. The love for her brother was different from what she had felt for her ex. Maybe she'd never truly loved Ralph. Maybe she had only needed him for a time.

"You're right—"

"Of course I'm right." Haley leaned forward and looked down at Gwen. "Not another mention of him on this trip. Deal?"

Gwen nodded.

"Say it."

"Deal," she said, sitting up.

College kids on spring break packed the beach. Some were playing with a football, a few drank—concoctions mixed with too much alcohol no doubt—

and others were simply at peace soaking up the sun's rays.

Gwen closed her eyes. The ocean and voices of the people on the beach became her soundtrack in the dark. The voices reminded her of a time when she was much younger and sat with her brother in the nurse's office at school. The chatter of young life had flooded the narrow halls as the two of them waited for one of their parents to fetch Thomas. Her brother had vomited in class. "Everything will be fine," she'd told him. Those words would turn out to be a lie. Later that week, they got the news that shattered their family.

Gwen intercepted a tear threatening to run down her cheek.

"Gwen, don't even think about him," Haley said. "He's an asshole."

"Yes," Gwen said. Haley scolding her over the wrong assumption that she was still thinking about her ex was easier to take than telling her friend that her brother was the one on her mind. Thinking about Thomas was difficult. Talking about him was impossible.

Gwen reached for her phone in the bag alongside her. She plugged her earphones in. "I'm going to listen to some music. If I fall asleep, wake me in twenty. I don't want to burn."

"Will do," Haley said, giving her the thumbs-up.

Gwen laid on her stomach and closed her eyes. The music replaced the sounds of the beach, but the beat took its time to clear her heavy mind. She didn't want to think about her ex or her brother, and her parents popped up in the fore of her thoughts. She couldn't help but wonder what they were doing.

Her mother had dropped her off at the airport, where she met up with Haley and some of Haley's other friends. The vacation had been a reward for her first successful year at college. Her father didn't agree with the trip, but he'd succumbed in the end. He had gotten together with her the day before she went to the airport. Her parents refused to be near each other since the divorce a few months after Thomas's passing. Neither of them even mentioned the other when she last saw them.

Gwen remembered when she started her college journey. Her father had dropped her off the first day. It had been a contentious decision with her mother initially wanting to, but her father had the pickup and was able to help her bring her stuff. Her mother came to see her the next day. A week later she met Ralph. He quickly filled in the cracks of her family life.

Now she was single.

The chorus in the song that played was one she knew well. It guided her to better memories. The warm sun soothed her strained shoulders.

Gwen welcomed the pull of sleep.

* * *

Opening her eyes, Gwen battled to come out of the haze. Being asleep meant an escape from feeling; being awake only brought truth and reality. A memory of a time she'd entered Thomas's room filled her mind's

150

eye. She had been unable to wake him and feared he was in a coma, or worse, dead. That time he did return from his slumber. The medication he had received to help him sleep made it difficult to come out of his state of rest.

Gwen swore under her breath as she removed her earphones, hating when painful memories snuck up on her. She expected to hear the hustle and bustle of life on the beach, but there were no voices or laughter. The ocean waves were clearly audible, however. She turned onto her side. Her back was warmer than she would have liked.

She wanted to ask Haley why she had let her burn, but her friend was gone. A scrunched-up towel covered in sand remained. Gwen checked her phone.

There was no signal.

Gwen sat up, noticing Haley's phone half covered in sand near the end of her towel. She picked up her friend's phone, wiping some of the dirt away and placed it in her handbag. The ocean filled her view as she lifted her gaze. Haley, she figured, must have gone to take a dip. It didn't sound like a bad idea: some cool water to alleviate the heat of the sun.

She didn't see Haley.

She saw no one.

Gwen stood and turned around. She was the only one on the beach, and it didn't compute. People don't vanish. Staring toward the road and some of the restaurants near the boardwalk, she saw no activity.

She looked back toward the ocean, and then to her sides again, just to be sure. What was going on?

An uncomfortable feeling draped over her like a heavy blanket on a humid day, forcing her into action. She marched down one side of the beach, intent on finding Haley. Maybe something had happened? Maybe she'd missed something while she slept? She considered the possibilities of a shark sighting or maybe even someone nearly drowning. Those sorts of events would draw people . . . but surely not everyone?

She ignored the towels scattered all over the beach. What became harder to ignore were the more valuable items. A cooler box sat unattended, filled with drinks. A set of keys lay on one of the towels, along with an expensive smartphone. Farther on, someone had even left a wallet behind. No, something wasn't right. She couldn't deny it. The scene looked as if people had just up and run, leaving everything behind. Why? What on earth would make people do that?

Before she could suffer a panic attack, she heard sounds other than the ocean. They were voices. Somehow they seemed angry, and the words were indecipherable. She focused, even closing her eyes as she tried to pinpoint where the noise came from. Up ahead, to the right, she guessed. She opened her eyes and narrowed her view, scanning the area where she believed the voices emanated from.

Gwen was right.

People crowded together in the distance. They stood in what looked like a giant circle. Something bad must have happened. Once more, she wondered if it had possibly been a shark attack—didn't the brochure they read mention warnings of bull sharks and tiger sharks?—or maybe someone had drowned. The current of concern rocked her heart, but it was fleeting. Her mind steadied, set at ease by knowing she wasn't alone after all. It was sad someone might be hurt or worse, but after waking up alone, she couldn't deny the relief that flooded her veins at the sight of other people. The two conflicting feelings made her dizzy, and the sand felt more like cushions than the granular material beneath her feet.

She kept moving toward the people, keeping one eye out for Haley.

The crowd was closer now, less than fifty yards. Something was wrong. One of the people turned to look at her. He was a tall, slender man, and blood covered his white shirt. The man appeared a pale blue, and his almost orange hair stood up like the characters in films who get electrocuted. His body was near skeletal; his head appeared to have lost flesh and was but a skull now, a blue skull.

He stretched out with his arms and grunted.

Other members of the crowd, seemingly intrigued by the man's actions, turned toward Gwen. She stopped dead in her tracks. All the people seemed to have the same unhealthy blue color and wild hair— although some had red, purple, or even yellow mops on their head—as the first man, and they were all covered in blood. The rest of the crowd joined the man in grunting and staring at her as if she was an intruder to their world.

Gwen's brain strained for answers, but nothing came. What was wrong with these people? They looked like victims of skin eating viruses, massive explosions or fires, and chemical warfare. How could that be? She thought of calling out to them, but the way they stared her down and made strange animal noises told her she would get no comprehensible replies. Gwen feared for Haley. She stepped back, hoping if she moved away the crowd would lose interest in her. She stepped back again. They were still grunting, but none had come forward.

It was working. Gwen continued her retreat.

The man hobbled toward her first; the rest of the crowd followed.

* * *

Gwen was running. She had turned and bolted as soon as the crowd came for her. The sand blurred beneath her feet. Heavy breathing, her own, had replaced the sounds of the ocean, and her lungs hurt when she inhaled. She hadn't looked back to see how far behind the strange people were. Fear kept her neck locked in place, and her eyes focused on the world ahead of her. There had to be someone who could help her. She told herself to keep running and not to slow down.

She couldn't keep running. Her calves and thighs burned; they began to feel heavier as she tried to counter her body's desire for a rest. No, she needed to get out of her perilous situation without the help of someone else, at least at first. Her brain lit up, searching for alternatives other than continuing to run along the beach. The increased mental processes helped alleviate the physical fatigue.

The road to her left drew her attention. This idea also didn't require her to extinguish the hope of finding someone who knew what was going on, and who could get her to safety. She cursed herself internally for not thinking of getting off the beach when she had more energy. The thought of glancing behind to see what kind of distance she'd put between herself and the strange people crossed her mind. She couldn't. The hideous decayed faces, blue skeletal bodies, and unnatural movements of those *things* made her gag.

Ignoring the bitter taste in her mouth, she followed a path off the beach. She had to steady her nerves, as every obstruction, be it an advertising board, a dumpster, or even a tree, was an obstacle that could hide one of the strange people. The path led her to a parking area. Abandoned vehicles, some with doors ajar, others with windows smashed, greeted her. How had she slept through all this? It must have been a great commotion and looked as if some war had broken out all around her.

Blood splatter covered most of the vehicles.

The earlier nap felt decades away.

Gwen decreased her pace to a brisk walk. She looked around, even daring to peek at the beach. She could see the crowd far in the distance. They didn't move too fast, which brought some relief. It still didn't help her escape. Maybe if she headed into the city, she would find officers and other people.

She was about to jog when a blue hand, sticking out from behind one of the parked vehicles, made her stop. An orange band was tied around the wrist. Haley had been wearing an orange band.

"No," Gwen said, walking toward the vehicle.

She stepped between the cars. The sight sent her reeling back.

"No, please, no." She let out a whimper.

Haley's body lay between the two vehicles. At least what remained of it; everything below her waist was gone. Guts, intestines, and blood had spilled out over the ground. Her friend's lifeless blue visage looked toward the heavens, as if praying for help that never came. She had no eyes and bite-size portions of flesh were missing from her corpse.

Haley's hand moved. It wasn't possible. No one could be alive after suffering such gruesome injuries. Haley opened her mouth and grunted, just as the people on the beach had done. Gwen stood frozen as she watched Haley trying to turn herself over. Every attempt was futile. This couldn't be happening. Maybe she had never woken from her nap and this was all a bad dream. Her mind yanked her from the haze of denying the reality she'd descended into.

There was no time to lose control.

The people from the beach were still coming.

A scratching sound followed by a dull *thud* came from her right. She looked away from her deceased friend, who seemed to have come back to life as some undead abomination. It was an insane thought, but it was all that allowed her to shift to her next problem. Someone came out from behind a red pickup. The person, an elderly male—at least, Gwen assumed that was what he'd once been; it was nearly impossible to tell, as his body had decayed almost beyond the point of recognition—was as blue as the crowd on the beach. His swollen eyes threatened to pop out of his face. He sneered, revealing a yellow smile missing some teeth. He grunted, and red-and-black bile ran from the corners of his mouth. He held a severed limb in his right hand. If not for the colorful butterfly tattoo on the pale blue foot, Gwen may not have realized it was Haley's leg.

"Oh my God." Gwen stepped back. Her voice sounded foreign to her, almost blasphemous in the world gone wrong.

The man groaned and dropped the leg. He had something else on his mind now. He reached out with both his arms, and Gwen knew what he was, what the people on the beach were.

Zombies.

The idea sounded surreal as the word echoed in her mind, but she had little doubt. Either way, having a name for them helped her focus against her current foe. They also shared many similarities to the undead in movies she and Thomas had watched growing up.

She was never a fan of the films but knew her brother felt better when she watched with him. If he had been alive, he would've known what to do. She remembered the video games he used to love playing. He had blasted zombies left and right on the screen. When he'd gotten really ill, their parents had both allowed him to stay up and play more than they ever had before. Gwen had often come to sit and watch him. She didn't like the games much, but it was rare to see her brother smile near the end. Yes, he would have known what to do in her current situation. Of this, Gwen had no doubt.

A cacophony of clangs and bangs invaded her sense of hearing, and then came the grunting. The sound was loud, far too loud to be only one or two of them.

She glanced around.

Zombies poured toward her from every street and every building. This wasn't some nightmare she would wake from. The lingering pain in her chest after seeing Haley, along with her sore leg muscles, confirmed her reality. Gwen took a few steps back, looking for a direction to start running. There were no options anywhere ahead of her toward the city. The beach had undead attackers coming from both sides. The ocean provided another barrier. Or did it? She was a good swimmer. Could she swim out and then up the shore until she found a clear area? Doubt sunk in. What if these monsters filled the entire coast? What if—

The zombie that had killed Haley ran at her. His desire for fresh meat had claimed supremacy.

Gwen turned back to the beach and ran.

When her feet met the golden sand once more, her pace slowed, and she could hear the zombies groaning and moaning all around her again. Their voices were higher pitched than earlier. They were losing their minds watching her, their prey, just out of their grasp. Their intent was clear, however. They meant to do her unspeakable harm.

She ran into the water. As soon as it was deep enough, she dived in and swam away from the land.

She prayed the zombies couldn't swim.

* * *

The zombies followed Gwen into the water as if summoned by Poseidon himself. She didn't let up and only glanced back once or twice as she kept swimming until she knew the ocean floor was a good depth beneath her feet. Then she turned back to watch her pursuers. When the water reached their waists, they struggled and flapped their arms all around them as if trapped in quicksand. Yet, still they came. The desire to get to her fueled them like a drug.

They started to disappear beneath the water. Once under, they didn't return. Gwen hoped they weren't moving stealthily beneath the unrelenting waves toward her. She couldn't resist. It was as if an anchor hung around her neck; she ducked her head below the surface.

There were no zombies near her.

Whatever was happening to them, they weren't coming for her. A shape moved beneath her feet before she could return her head to the surface. It wasn't one of the undead. No, it was too big. A tail with a fin trailed the creature.

She knew the shape.

It was a shark.

The blood that covered the zombies must have attracted it, not to mention the flesh that appeared to be dropping off the undead in snack-size bites. A new terror was born within her mind. It wasn't the zombies she feared now. Raising her head above the water, she looked around. Another fin was visible not too far from her. It headed for the shore, for the undead, who kept coming in after her, not realizing that jagged and sharp teeth awaited them beneath the ocean. In the battle of sharks versus zombies, there would only be one winner.

As Gwen floated, trying to process what to do, another memory infiltrated her mind. When Thomas had suffered serious pain from his illness, their parents had tried aquatic therapy. It worked wonders initially. After a session, Thomas would be close to his old self for the remainder of the day. She remembered how much he loved the ocean when he was much younger, before the illness. Gwen no longer had the same appreciation for the ocean. She would be content if she never saw another beach again.

Something moved in her peripheral vision to her left. A large fin stuck out above the water. The shark headed to the zombies like the others she had seen. Gwen was too close for comfort. This area was going to become a kill zone.

She swam to her right, always fearful of coming across another shark.

Gunshots rang out. They were rapid-fire, not single-shot. It sounded like the war documentaries her father used to watch when she was younger.

She tried to focus beyond the beach.

What could be going wrong now?

* * *

Hope.

It wasn't an illusion. It was real. Groups of men and women dressed in military gear opened fire on the zombies. Like in the battle against the sharks, the undead stood no chance. This wasn't like a movie, where the zombies got to overrun everything. The soldiers appeared trained and prepared. Their bullets tore limbs off. The zombies that hadn't become food for the sharks fell in dismembered piles all over the beach. Blood ran freely, turning the sand a dark red.

Gwen's heart beat as if it had found another gear. She had to get back to the shore. The soldiers could save her. She needed to get to them before they moved off somewhere else. Surely they would know where any survivors could go to be safe from whatever hell had broken out.

Fearful of the sharks feasting at the zombie buffet, Gwen decided to swim a wide berth back to shore. She forced herself to look beneath her every few strokes, to check for any large shapes in her vicinity. It wasn't easy. Her mind would have preferred to pretend there were no sharks and that she was taking a leisurely swim. Gwen knew better and fought through the fatigue while trying to keep her strokes consistent.

Something tapped the underside of her foot.

The idea that a shark or zombie would pull her under when she was so near the shore hurt like a blade to the heart. Gwen lowered her head into the water, bracing for whatever foe came her way.

There was no shark. There was no zombie.

Her foot had touched the ground.

She exhaled. Knowing she could stand, she placed both feet down. It felt odd to have ground beneath her. The time adrift had seemed like an eternity. She raised one of her arms above her head, trying to wave the tired limb to attract the attention of one of the soldiers on the beach. She stumbled to a group of them.

The last few steps back to the beach were the hardest. She stopped as soon as the water was below her knees.

"Over here, over here!" one of the soldiers shouted.

"Help," Gwen muttered. Her voice was weak, surprising her. She wanted to scream but knew she was running on fumes. The exhaustion revealed itself now as safety numbed the terror she'd experienced. Gwen had escaped zombies and sharks, monsters on the land and monsters in the sea, on the same day. Not many people could say that. The nightmare was over. It was wonderful to see fellow human beings. Good, normal, caring creatures who didn't want to eat her. The tingling in her core was overwhelming. She wanted to cry as two of the soldiers made their way toward her.

"Miss, are you okay?" one of the soldiers asked.

"I'm—" Gwen couldn't get any more words out. All she could think of to do was nod. The fatigue lowered her internal defenses, and it was clear she had never loved Ralph. The breakup hadn't actually been that hard. She'd merely used it as a way to feel miserable to keep other unresolved issues at bay. The wall she had built within came crumbling down, and Gwen realized she'd never gotten over the loss of her brother. When she got home, she decided she would help her parents communicate with one another again. They would talk about Thomas. They would remember Thomas. It would be the best way for her family to heal. Then maybe she could move forward with her life.

A gunshot echoed across the now silent beach.

Heat exploded in Gwen's chest.

"Why did you shoot her?" She heard the one soldier ask the other.

"Orders," the other replied. "We can't risk infection, or the knowledge of what happened here getting out."

Gwen's body tipped backward. The sky rushed before her eyes, and then came a splash as she landed on her back in shallow water. Yes, she had survived two different monsters today, but she couldn't survive the actions of her fellow man. No, she wouldn't see her parents again. Her life in this world cut short like her brother's.

It was okay.

She would have more time to spend with Thomas in the next realm.

SHE WILL RISE

* * *

Luna Mendes's mother, Selma, lay inert in the bed. Her thinning gray hair fell over the side of her face like the spiderwebs Luna recalled from the attic of their first home. They had left that house when Luna's father died from a heart attack. She was only four at the time and didn't remember much about him. She did, however, remember his pale skin when he had fallen ill the last few months before his death. Her mother's ashen face now reminded her of her father.

Selma's forearms, not covered by the pink shirt she wore, were barely more than bones. Her gaunt face and deep-set eyes made her seem much older than her forty-three years. Luna couldn't believe how fast her mother had deteriorated since she was last at home.

"You sure I can't make you anything to eat?" Luna asked.

"No, thank you." Selma tried to look up at her daughter. The strain was evident in her wrinkled forehead. "I'm just a bit tired this evening. We have all weekend to spend together. I'm excited to hear how college is going."

"Of course," Luna said, taking a step away from the bed. "I'll tell you all about it in the morning."

Selma didn't reply. Her eyes had closed.

Luna walked out of the room, gently closing the door behind her. She made her way to the bedroom she and her sister had shared for so many years.

Posters no longer covered the walls, and the second bed was also gone, though they'd removed that three years ago, after her sister, Isabella, had died. A drunk driver had struck her while she was walking home from the store. The room intensified the feelings of loss.

Luna reached into her pocket for the faded photograph of her sister she always carried. It didn't do Isabella's beauty justice, but it was still Luna's favorite picture of her. It was also the only photo she had of Isabella with her hair the purple color she'd dyed it days after turning fifteen. Their mother had been furious.

They had been twins and would have been nineteen and at college now. Luna often tried to picture what Isabella would've looked like if she were still alive. Sometimes Luna stood before a mirror and imagined herself with different hair and the colorful, eccentric clothes her sister loved, as if that would give her a glimpse of the sibling who should've been.

Luna turned the photograph over to see Isabella's scribbled note—*five tips to an awesome life*—on the back. The fifth tip, though, remained unwritten. Luna often wondered what it meant to say and usually made something up whenever she needed advice or guidance in her life.

A loud *clang* came from the living room, reminding Luna she was home for the weekend. The sound must've been her mother's boyfriend, Ralph; he likely sat in his tattered chair with a beer. Luna regretted coming home for Easter, but her mother was ill, and Luna didn't like that she was alone with Ralph all the time. She flinched at the image of him. The greasy long hair, the perpetual stench of sweat hovering around him, and the crooked yellow smile caused an undertow of melancholy within her as a shiver crept down her back. If she didn't think of more pleasant things, the undertow would become tidal waves of hate, unrelenting as they beat on the shore of her mind.

It wasn't easy to remove him from her thoughts.

He had hit her mother once.

Luna had been over at friend's house when it happened, but she saw the bruised cheek for the next two weeks. He had never laid a hand on her, but he'd called her many derogatory names. Luna clenched her fingers tight into a fist. She stretched out her fingers and inhaled deeply. She turned the photo back to her sister and held it up close to her eyes; the anger within calmed.

She wanted to do something nice for her mother, like take her somewhere, but Selma was too ill to go out. An idea surfaced: Luna would cook one of her mother's favorite meals. After the hardships of the last few years, her mother deserved some good holiday memories. She headed to the kitchen to have a look and see what ingredients she'd need to buy in the morning.

Ralph belched as she entered the living room. Otherwise, he did nothing to indicate that he realized she existed. His eyes remained fixated on the low-budget action movie on the screen before him. He took a sip of his beer.

"Ah, for fuck's sake." Ralph groaned, dropping the empty beer bottle onto the floor alongside him. "Hey, sweetie," he said to Luna, "don't you want to pass me another beer from the fridge?"

Luna did exist after all, at least when Ralph wanted something. It wasn't the first time he had asked her to fetch him a beer. She hated every time he did.

"Now, Luna," Ralph said. "I'm an old man. Have some compassion, you filthy witch."

Luna didn't respond. She remembered Isabella's first tip on the back of the photo: *ignore assholes.* There was no bigger asshole than Ralph. Instead of responding, she fetched a bottle of beer and brought it to him. She paused, a step behind him, and held the beer like a club. She forced herself to take another step forward and eased her hold on the beverage.

He snatched the beer but didn't thank her.

She had gone back to not existing.

Luna chose to forego her idea of checking what ingredients she'd require until morning, and she escaped to the bedroom. She exhaled when she gripped the back of a chair in the room. The desire to smash the bottle over Ralph's skull had lingered longer than usual.

Isabella would never have allowed Ralph to date their mother.

* * *

When Luna woke the following morning, she was eager to check on her mother. She traversed the narrow passageway to her mother's bedroom. An icy shiver trailed over her back as she thought of running into Ralph, but the fear wasn't necessary. She had heard his pickup drive off a few minutes ago. If she was totally honest, she'd lain in bed waiting for him to get up and walk past her room. That he had left to go somewhere was a bonus.

"Come in," her mother said, her voice raspy, when Luna knocked.

Luna opened the bedroom door and entered.

Her mother looked a bit better. She was lying with her back propped up against the bed's headboard, with a pillow behind her head.

"Come sit next to me." Selma patted the bed next to her.

Luna cringed internally. That was the side Ralph slept on. Instead of sitting there, she walked to the other side of the bed, where she leaned against a dresser.

"How are you feeling?" Luna asked.

"Better, especially now that I see you." A fleeting smile trailed Selma's words.

"I was thinking last night—what if I helped out tomorrow? Maybe I could prepare lunch for us. It's Easter, after all. We should enjoy the weekend."

"No, you should be relaxing. College isn't easy. Ralph has been cooking since I've been ill. I'm sure he could—"

"I want to do it." Luna couldn't help but remember Isabella's second tip on the back of the photo: *care for family*. Luna was trying to, at least in respect to her mother.

"That's kind of you, Luna. Ralph and I would appreciate it. What do you need?"

Luna doubted Ralph would appreciate anything other than maybe a truckload of booze, and even that might bring only ephemeral gratitude. "I'll head to the store in a bit."

"Ralph could pick up what you want. He's at his friend Donny's this morning. I could call—"

"No, Mother." Luna placed her hand on her mother's shoulder, not wanting to come across as too direct. It was Ralph she didn't like. Her venom should be reserved for him. "I want to go to town."

Selma nodded. "Oh, you should check out the old videotapes we have of Isabella while you're here. You used to watch them for hours after, after—"

Luna reached out and held her mother's hand. "It's okay. I miss her, too."

She put on a brave face. The old tapes hit a nerve, but her mother was right. She had spent many hours viewing the footage of her sister. Maybe she and her mother could even sit and watch some of the videos together tomorrow. Warmth swelled within her. The eagerness to fast-forward to the desired moment the next day was potent.

"I'll go sort through them. Are they still in the living room?"

Selma shook her head. "Ralph put them somewhere else. He needed space for his DVDs."

"All right. You get some more rest. Maybe once I've found them and returned from town, you'll feel even better."

Luna kissed her mother's forehead and then exited the room, closing the door behind her. She wouldn't have to wait long to ask Ralph where the tapes were, as she heard him slam his pickup door by the time she entered the living room. His trip to his friend hadn't lasted as long as Luna would've liked. Having had an hour or two to build some courage to ask him for the tapes would've been preferable.

When Ralph entered, he was clutching a beer as if it were the most valuable item he had ever owned. He frowned when he saw Luna standing, waiting for him. He took a sip, trying to look beyond Luna as he walked past her.

"Ralph, I was wondering if you knew where the old videotapes are."

Ralph turned to face her, grinned, and then scratched his nose. "Yeah, I threw them away."

The words felt as if they went straight through Luna's head. "In one ear, out the other," as her mother would say. She simply couldn't believe them, but she knew it wasn't a joke. Ralph didn't make jokes unless they were vile and offensive. "I'm sorry, Ralph. What did you say?"

"Are you deaf? I said I threw them away."

"Why would you do that?" Luna stepped back. She had raised her voice, which was never a good thing to do around Ralph.

He took another sip from his beer. "Fuck's sake. They're old shit. DVDs are much better—that is, until I get my Blu-ray setup sorted. Why the fuck would you want shitty VHS tapes? Next you'll be asking for records."

Luna kept quiet. Even though the anger raged within her like a volcano threatening to explode, she knew Ralph was reaching his own tipping point. All the signs were there: the reddening face, the pouted lips, and the way he pushed his chest out.

"I asked you a question." Ralph stepped toward her. "What the fuck is wrong with you?"

"Nothing," Luna whispered.

Ralph slapped her across the face. The blow was powerful and lightning fast. Luna didn't have time to move, raise her hands, or even flinch. It sent her reeling backward, and she fell on her rear. The old tan carpet did nothing to soften her landing.

"Wrong answer," Ralph said. Again, he turned away from her as if she didn't exist.

Luna waited for him to leave the room, and then she got up, trying to stem the shaking of her hands. She made her way back to her room, ignoring the pulsating pain that had invaded her face, and locked the door behind her. She needed a moment alone before heading to town and crawled into bed, where she buried her face in the pillow.

She smothered her tears.

* * *

The next day, Luna chose not to mention anything to her mother about Ralph hitting her. She didn't want to cause trouble, especially with her mother being ill. It was Sunday, and her last day at home. Maybe if her mother's health improved, Luna could talk to her and try to get her to see Ralph for what he was. She hadn't yet. What would make her change now? Would Ralph slapping Luna really make a difference? Probably not, considering Luna knew Ralph had hit her mother before, even if it was a while ago—at least, she *believed* it was the last and only time he'd done it. She hadn't seen any new bruises on her mother. Doubts were creeping in. Regardless, her mother was still with him. She would have to accept this fact for the rest of the weekend, at least.

Luna tried to get Ralph out of her mind, but it was difficult. He snored from the bedroom. There was good news, though. Selma appeared brighter and sat in the living area with a multicolored blanket covering her legs.

Luna began placing all the necessary ingredients on the kitchen counter. Not only was she making them lunch, but she also had plans for dessert. If only she could find the whisk. Scanning the top cupboard and the drawers resulted in nothing. She got onto her knees and checked the cupboard beneath the sink.

There were a few empty beer cans, crushed, and an empty beer bottle or two, but nothing else. No, there was something else. A box behind one of the pipes caught her eye, and she brought it out of the cupboard. Rat poison? Why would they have rat poison? They'd never had rats. Luna shook her head, trying to understand. It hit her.

Ralph was poisoning her mother.

Maybe he wanted the house all for himself. Maybe he only wanted her weak. The thought of him poisoning her mother stuck, even though a voice within Luna's mind told her it was surely madness. It was easy to mute the voice. She hated Ralph. Any reason to add gasoline to the fire was welcome, but it would also explain her mother's illness the last few months. If her mother's doctor couldn't detect anything wrong, maybe they hadn't been checking for the right problem: poison.

Luna marched into the living room. "What's this?"

Her mother looked up, straining her eyes at the box. "I don't know. What is it?"

"It's rat poison."

"But we don't have rats."

"I know." Luna sighed. "I found it in one of the kitchen cupboards. Who did you say has been making all your meals lately?"

"Ralph. But what does—"

"He's been poisoning you. He was probably too scared to do it while I've been home. That's why you're doing better."

Selma put her hand up, as if trying to block a punch. "No, no, I'm sure it must be for something else. Ralph would never—"

"Ralph is an asshole." Luna tossed the rat poison onto the sofa alongside her mother. She remembered the third of Isabella's tips: *stand up for those who can't*. Luna wouldn't only stand up for her mother, she would die for her. If Ralph was poisoning her, he would regret—

"What did you say?"

Luna turned. Ralph stood next to her with disgust etched into his face. His nostrils flared.

"No, no," Selma said. "Ralph, it's just a misunderstanding."

"Misunderstanding? This bitch called me an asshole." He raised his hand as he had done the previous day.

Luna braced herself, expecting the searing heat of the blow. Ralph didn't slap her. He punched her. The shot landed on the side of her jaw.

Her knees buckled as she fell sideways from the hit. She landed on her hip and heard her mother shouting at Ralph.

"You shut the fuck up," he said. "This girl needs a good lesson."

Luna crawled away.

Ralph tried to clamp down on her calf and then her ankle. His hand felt rough and greasy.

She escaped the unwanted touch and jumped to her feet.

Her mother was crying hysterically, but was still too weak to move without help. Ralph had a wild look in his eyes, as if he wasn't going to stop at a lesson. Fear circulated throughout Luna's body like electricity, and she exploded past Ralph. He didn't expect her movement and failed to get his arms up in time to grab her.

Luna ran into the kitchen, where she swung the back door open.

Ralph's footsteps were just behind her.

Tears streaked her cheeks as she bolted into the backyard.

* * *

The bright light of the day made everything appear as if it were in slow motion. Luna scanned the backyard, looking for an escape; tall trees at the perimeter of the yard filled her view. The woods weren't deep, but there was no way she would be able to outrun Ralph all the way to the . . . cemetery. Yes, the local cemetery was beyond the woods. It was where they had buried Isabella.

This realization that her sister was in close proximity imbued her with a newfound strength. She turned around to face Ralph. The fourth of Isabella's tips—*get the truth*—played as if from a loudspeaker in her head.

Ralph seemed taken aback that she had stopped and was no longer running. He paused a few feet from her and stared her down. "What you going to do?"

Luna didn't know, but she knew what she wanted. "I want you to admit that you've been poisoning my mother. I want the truth, no bullshit. Then I want you to pack your bags and leave, before I call the cops. I never want to see you again."

Ralph chuckled and showed her the middle finger.

Luna stepped back, glancing from side to side. She realized she was subconsciously looking for a weapon. The ax stuck into a pile of wood, a pile Ralph had still not gotten around to chopping in over a year, stood out like a fire in the night. It was only a few feet from her. She needed to catch Ralph off guard.

"Don't even think about," Ralph said, stepping toward the ax.

"Tell me the truth, Ralph." He had foiled her plan to get the weapon, but it didn't stop her inner desire demanding he admit what he'd been doing.

Ralph snickered. "Have you lost your fucking mind? Who do you think will pay the bills if I'm not around?"

"Anything will be better than having you around."

Before Ralph could reply, there was a loud *crack*. The sound was similar to thunder, but it came from the woods. Luna wanted to look but was afraid to take her eyes off Ralph. The weather had also changed. A wind had started up and whistled through the trees behind her, as if her last words awoke Mother Nature. When she felt the sudden chill in the air, she couldn't stop the gooseflesh from breaking out all over her arms.

"Step back, Luna. I have this under control," a woman from behind her said. The voice sounded so familiar. Still, Luna didn't look back. Ralph was too unpredictable and too dangerous to forget about, if even for a moment. She focused on him instead, waiting for the stranger to come into view and hoping they would help.

Ralph was staring past her. His eyes threatened to pop out of his head, and his mouth was wide open, exposing his poorly cared for teeth. "It-it's not possible."

Luna couldn't resist. She turned around.

Isabella came out from the line of trees.

Dirt covered Isabella's white dress. Her skin was pale, whiter than even the cleanest area on the dress. Her eyes were black as night. She marched toward the two of them as if she were ferromagnetic material pulled by a magnetic field.

Luna couldn't believe it. A flurry of different emotions circled inside of her. It was only when she heard Ralph say, "Get out of here. You freak. You're dead," that she realized he still posed a threat to her. As Isabella continued toward them, unconcerned with anything Ralph said, Luna saw that her sister held an ax in one hand.

Luna looked toward the large stack of wood.

The ax she had sought moments ago was gone.

* * *

It could only be described as an out-of-body experience—a feeling of weightlessness, as if gravity no longer applied, and then a tingling sensation spreading through the body, followed by complete nothingness. No, time hadn't stood still. She was still in danger. What she saw wasn't an illusion, or was it?

Luna's mind, hoping to hold on to her before she broke from her tether to reality, played three facts over on a loop. On the first day home, she had found her mother was much more ill than she'd feared. On the second day, Ralph hit her. On the third, her sister rose from the grave. It was difficult to accept all three of these truths.

Ralph helped. He stepped forward and pushed her out of the way. His concern now was Isabella.

For the second time that day, Luna fell onto the ground. She crooked her neck, surveying the surreal scene. Isabella was now right before Ralph, who had a new look carved into his face. Luna watched perplexed, as she'd never seen this expression on him before.

Fear, that's what it was.

Luna looked to her sister and couldn't resist asking, "How did you—"

Isabella held her hand up at Luna, and with the other hand, she raised the ax.

Ralph readied his fists. "Fuck—"

The ax's blade landed in Ralph's right shoulder. Blood spurted into the air as if he had turned into a sprinkler shooting raspberry-colored liquid. From Luna's perspective, it shimmered as it flew across the blue sky. Was Ralph screaming? It sounded like it, but Luna couldn't be sure as her senses still didn't function right after seeing her sister. Isabella swung the ax again, this time she aimed for Ralph's chest.

Ralph fell backward. Unlike when she had fallen earlier, Luna knew he'd never get up again. He surprised her by reaching up with one arm as he lay on his back. Blood exited his mouth and nose. The ax remained lodged in his chest.

"He's still alive." Luna stood.

"Don't worry," Isabella said. "He's as good as gone. Let him suffer a bit. He doesn't deserve mercy."

"But he's still a—"

"Everything will be okay, Luna."

The words were reassuring. Luna suddenly had no doubt everything *would* be okay. Her sister was always right. Worrisome thoughts dissipated. The feelings she had for her sister and mother claimed supremacy within her. "You saved us. You came back to save us."

"You were always the strongest, Luna." Isabella grabbed Ralph's hands. "Look at all you've accomplished so far. And you have so much more to do.”

“You can’t stay?”

“I’m afraid not.”

“Will I ever see you again?”

Isabella shook her head. “It took much for me to come this once, but you won’t need me again. You’ve risen into someone powerful. You’re starting to realize it now. I see it in your eyes.”

“I’ve missed you.”

“I’ve missed you too,” Isabella said, dragging Ralph backward to the woods, “but now you must go and take care of Mom. I’ll take care of him.”

Luna watched with pain in her heart. It was true; she did feel different. Something inside her had awoken during the weekend. Isabella was almost at the perimeter of the yard, just moments from disappearing into the woods, when a thought popped into Luna’s mind.

“Isabella,” Luna called after her sister, “what was the fifth tip? On the back of the photo when you dyed your hair purple.”

“I remember that.” Isabella paused, looking at Ralph. “The fifth tip is stop any motherfuckers who intend to do you or your family harm.”

It made perfect sense to Luna, and she burned the tip into her mind, eager to write it down as soon as she could.

Isabella took another step toward the woods.

“Wait,” Luna said.

Luna ran to her sister, and then snatched the ax out from Ralph's chest. She yanked on his collar, pulling him free from Isabella's hold. He was still alive, but choking on his own blood.

Luna aimed for his neck.

The ax didn't go straight through, the way she'd seen in movies, but Luna persevered. The hatred poured out of her heart, down her arms into her hands, and then out through the ax. She needed it all out and lost count of how many times she swung the ax, but she knew it was many, as her forearms, biceps, and shoulders burned like never before. Blood spurted up into the air; some drops hit her in the face. The crimson substance smelled wonderful, rivaling the best perfumes. It tasted sweeter than honey as she licked the corners of her mouth. Yes, there was no doubt something had awoken within her. She'd risen. She would never fall again.

Finally, the ax separated head from body.

"There you go," Isabella said. "Do you feel better now?"

"May I keep the ax?"

"Why? He's dead now, Luna."

"For when mom gets better, in case she meets another asshole, or—"

"Or?"

"Or if I ever do."

PROM SCREAMS

William Carlson passed the money to the short, stocky man with the dirty beard and black baseball cap. Four hundred dollars for a couple of hours seemed ridiculous. What else could he do? He had run out of options and wanted to upstage all his friends. Plus, it wasn't as if he was hurting for cash with his father owning almost ten percent of the property in town. The man checked the bills, scrunched his nose, and then indicated for William to wait outside the dilapidated apartment building.

This left him alone, and it was night in a seedy part of town. Trying to take his mind off his location, he glanced at his wristwatch. Time was against him. He still needed to drive all the way across town. A few days ago, after his girlfriend dumped him right before the prom, the new plans he had made seemed like a great idea. Now, his stomach twisted and turned as if a royal rumble match headlined in his intestines.

A *creak* alerted him to the door opening.

The man came out alone, which didn't help ease the tension in William's core. He expected to see Svetlana, the girl he had selected. He'd emailed her all week, providing her with info so she would know how to play it if his friends asked too many questions tonight.

"There's a minor hiccup," the man said. "Svetlana isn't feeling so good. She's kind of passed out at the moment. Don't worry. It happens from time to time."

"Don't worry?" The tension knotted within him. Anger seeped from its grasp. "I need to get going, *now*."

"Svetlana's not going to be ready to go anywhere for at least another hour or so."

"You've got to be kidding me."

"Relax, kid. You don't want to do something stupid." The man crooked his mouth into an awkward smile. "You think you're such a big shot. Maybe I can help you out. I have this other girl, one who wasn't working tonight. For an extra hundred she's all yours."

William curled his hands into tight fists, but he was out of options. He released his frustration and pulled out his wallet. The man snatched the extra hundred as soon as he held it out. "How am I supposed to teach her everything she needs to remember?"

"Not my problem."

William shook his head. The night was already tricky. He didn't need any added complications.

"But hey." The volume of the man's voice dropped, and he moved nearer to William. "She's a bit different. Don't get too close to this one for too long."

"What's that supposed to mean?"

"Figure it out, kid."

The man entered the building. He took longer than his first trip inside, but this time he came out with a young woman.

Her pale skin glowed underneath the light above the door, and her hair blended tones of red and orange, reminding William of a fire blazing. She scanned him with green eyes, and then looked to the night. She was beautiful, far more captivating and younger than the images he had seen of Svetlana. William guessed her age to be nineteen or twenty. She also fit the part in her body-hugging yellow dress and white heels. At least his friends would be even more jealous once they saw her.

"This is Fay," the man said.

William shook her hand. "Hi, I'm William."

"Nice to meet you, William. I'm Fay."

"Yeah. I got that. We'd best—"

"You have her back by midnight," the man commanded. "Or there'll be shit. You got me, kid? This girl is special. At midnight I turn into a wild animal, and you don't want me to have to come find you."

"Yeah, man. I'll have her back."

"And you treat her well. You hear me?"

William didn't have time to waste. He nodded and led Fay to his vehicle. The story would need to be simple for her to remember, because the last thing he wanted to endure was his friends catching him out. No money in the world would cure that embarrassment.

When she climbed in, he realized he had forgotten to open the door for her. He ceased the thought. There were greater concerns now. He started the engine, eager to get out of the shady neighborhood.

"Do you know why I hired you?"

"Can we play some music? I love listening to music in the car. Don't you?"

"No. You need to listen to me. Didn't that moron tell you why I was hiring you for the night?"

"Oh," Fay said, gazing out her window. "You need a girlfriend."

"Hey. I need you to focus. Look at me."

Fay turned to him, twirling the ends of her hair.

"It's not so simple," William said. "I need you to pretend like we've hung out a few times. We're going to my prom and all my friends will be there. I'll give you some info on how we met and some stuff about me. Okay?"

"Okay."

"Right, so, I'm an only child. I—" William paused. Fay stared out the window again, head tilted up at the sky.

"Hey." William tapped the dashboard. "Are you listening to me?"

"Are you going to play music now?"

"Fuck me."

"I don't do that. But one of the other girls—"

"Stop," William said, holding his hand up. "Let's start over. I'm going to tell you our cover story. Okay?"

"I love stories. Tales about werewolves, ghosts, vampires, aliens, and witches are some of my favorite."

William bit down on his tongue.

* * *

They drove near the center of town, where a few of the bars, a nightclub, and some other shadier joints lined the streets. William ignored the clock ticking in his mind. He had managed to get some details through to Fay, while confusing himself once or twice when he muddled his facts and lies. He persisted.

"So how long have we been together?" William asked.

"One week."

"No," William said, shaking his head. "That's too short. I said three weeks. You need to listen. I—"

"I need to stop at work."

"What?"

"I need to stop at work. I've forgotten something important."

"There's no time. We're already going to be late."

"Please." Fay placed her hand on William's arm. "I have to get something at work."

Her touch warmed his arm. Her eyes focused on his. This was the most she had paid attention to anything, and William couldn't resist her gaze.

"What do you need?"

"Please, William. It's my medication."

William sighed. "Okay. Shit. But we better be fast. Where do you work?"

"Bad Girls Go Everywhere."

"The strip club?"

"Yes. It's just up the road."

"I know where it is."

"You've been there? I've never seen you before."

"No, I haven't been inside. I know of the place." William applied pressure to the gas pedal. The sign for the club stood out against others up ahead. He searched the darkened lot for an empty parking space.

Once they parked, Fay wasted no time getting out of the vehicle. William wasn't going to sit and wait. He wanted to make sure she was quick, so he followed her. Approaching the building, William encountered two large men wearing black suits. Both men had shaved heads and showed no emotion.

"He's with me," Fay said to the men.

The men nodded, but stared William down as he passed them.

Entering the club, William walked through a cloud of smoke. He inhaled the overwhelming stench of cigarettes and cigars. Hints of perfume and sweat came with his next breath. The lighting was poor except at a large stage up front, where colorful spotlights worshipped a woman wearing a G-string and nurse's cap. She held a stethoscope over the bare chest of a middle-aged man who sat bound with rope to a chair.

Fay passed another big guy in a suit. This one, however, had a black ponytail. "He's with me," she said to the man as she entered a room.

William followed her into a long, narrow dressing area. A large rectangular mirror covered most of the wall to his right. Women took over his view. Two seated right by him were topless, applying makeup. Another two walked ahead of him, completely naked, though the blonde to the left stopped to put on a pink G-string. William stood mesmerized. It wasn't often he walked into a room filled with beautiful naked women. For a moment, he forgot what he was doing.

Fay reappeared. "Let's go," she said, clutching a large black handbag. "I got my medication."

"Yeah. Okay."

William stole a final glance at the women before turning around. They all smiled and a few waved at him. He made a mental note to come back to the club one day.

A tall, pale man with a bald head awaited Fay when they exited the room. He crooked his neck, narrowing his eyes at her. "Inferno, I didn't know you were on tonight. I mean, they said you weren't, but I thought I'd stick around to be sure."

"Oh, okay." Fay stepped back. "No, I'm not working."

"Who is this?" the man asked, glancing at William.

"I'm helping him out."

"But—but you told me you don't go home with customers."

"I don't."

The ponytailed guy from earlier came and stood alongside Fay. "Is everything okay over here?" he asked, pushing his chest out while holding his right fist in his left hand.

"Yes." Fay turned. "I'll see you soon. I've got some shows next week," she said to the bald man. "I have to get going now."

There was something off about Baldy, what William named the man in his thoughts, and it wasn't only his peculiar demeanor. A beam of light from the stage briefly shone across Baldy. William tried not to react to his appearance in the light. Burn scars covered the left side of his face and neck. The man wore a long-sleeve shirt and pants; black gloves hid his hands.

Fay pulled on William's arm, gently, but strongly enough that he followed her. Baldy hadn't seemed pleased at all. William ignored the concern, however, and walked with Fay back through the dimly lit club.

"Why did he call you Inferno?" William asked, stepping into the cool night air.

"It's my stage name. I do a show with fire. You should come see it one night. It's very popular."

"I will. Who was that guy?"

"He's a customer. He watches a lot of my shows."

"And, um, what happened to him?"

Fay stared up at the night sky. "He got too close once."

"Damn. Okay."

"It wasn't my fault. He was drunk and came up on stage."

"That's crazy."

Fay punched him on the arm. It wasn't hard, but it wasn't too soft either. "It wasn't my fault."

"Okay." William held his hands up. "It wasn't your fault."

* * *

Back on the road, William repeated the cover story he wanted Fay to remember. She seemed to be listening this time. The strange man had rattled her, and her mind didn't stray from the present. With all the detours behind him, William returned his concerns to the prom. They would be thirty minutes late, but it was okay. He would have a girl hotter than any of his friends' dates. At least that's what he told himself.

"Excellent," William said when Fay answered another of his questions correctly. She had remembered both his parents' names, what he wanted to do for a career, and his dog's name. He had to make up names for her parents, as she refused to give theirs. He also told her she had a cat named Tinker Bell, which she called "Tink" for short.

"Right," William said, pretending his finger was a gun and firing at the windshield. "What should we go over next?"

"I have these strange episodes. I can also do weird things at times. That's why I needed my medication."

"Are you being serious or trying to add to the cover story?" William frowned. "I think we need solid information. We don't need too much other stuff; otherwise, we'll get confused."

"I'm being serious."

"I don't have to know any real weird stuff about you. It's not important."

"Okay. I was just—"

"Listen." William tapped on the wheel. "Let's keep this nice and easy from here on out. I'll even throw in a bonus hundred for you if you pull this off. Cool?"

"Can I smoke? I don't like to really, but it does calm me sometimes."

"But we'll stink."

Fay didn't reply.

"Ah, fine." William rolled down her window. "There, do what you have to do. Blow the shit outside. It's bad for your health, you know."

Fay reached into her handbag, pulling out a pack of smokes and a lighter. She lit a cigarette and inhaled. William focused on the road. The school was near. The night had started off a bit odd, but things were getting better.

"Ha-choo."

"Bless you," William said, turning to Fay.

She patted the dashboard. A little flame flickered behind her hand. "I'm sorry. That happens sometimes."

"What the hell are you doing? Why did you light the dash on fire?"

"I didn't do it on purpose." Fay killed the flame. A puff of smoke trailed its demise but quickly dissipated. "It happens sometimes when I sneeze."

"Don't talk shit to me. What are you, a dragon? I'm the one who has to get that repaired." William tried to keep one eye on the road while also making sure Fay wasn't up to anything else. "What was that medication you had to get at the club? It better not be drugs of any kind."

"It's medication, I swear. I told you I have a condition." Fay opened her handbag. "I better take it now, just in case."

"In case of what?"

"It's not here. It has to be." She dumped her handbag out on the floor before her. "We have to go back."

"No way. Fay, you're fine. There's nothing wrong with you, physically at least. If you do get ill or something, we can always leave. Does that work for you?"

Fay sighed. "I hope I don't have any more symptoms."

"You'll be fine."

Fay rested her head on the window.

William shook his head. Being with Fay reminded him of a roller coaster. The ups and downs were ridiculous. His concern over how she would act at the party grew, but it was too late to change tack. If he didn't go with her, it would mean staying away. That wasn't an option. He had been excited for prom all year. Why did his ex have to dump him days before? It felt calculated, as if she wanted him to squirm. He smiled when he imagined the expression on her face when he walked in there with Fay. That would teach her.

Buoyed by the new thoughts, he said, "So how long ago did we meet?"

"Are we doing this again?"

"Yes. I'm paying for your time, after all. Now answer."

"I'm tired of it."

"Please."

Fay sighed. "We met three weeks ago."

* * *

William calculated they'd arrive at least forty-five minutes after prom started. His earlier assessment had been incorrect. He didn't mind so much, as arriving fashionably late might work to his advantage. Fay was nailing the cover story perfectly, and the more time he spent with her, the more her beauty infatuated him. His friends and ex would be falling over themselves soon enough. Some of her strange rambling did linger in the back of his mind though.

"I need to stop for a moment." Fay wound down the passenger window and stuck her head out.

"What? Why?" William hoped she wasn't going to smoke again.

"I don't feel well. This also happens sometimes. It's another symptom, but it will pass. Maybe getting outside will help."

"Doesn't the open window help?"

"No."

Her cheeks were rather red. William eased off the gas. He resisted grinding his teeth. The school was only another two blocks away. A moment to make sure he looked good before they arrived wasn't such a bad idea, or so he convinced himself. He parked the car near a large white double-story home shrouded in darkness.

"Okay," he said, "but let's not be more than a minute or—"

Fay took her heels off, opened the door, and hopped out. She didn't stand on the pavement to breathe in the night air as William expected. Instead, she made her way to a steel gate at the side of the house. Fay pulled on the gate, but it didn't budge. She raised a leg and placed her foot on one of the hinges. She reached up, gripped a bar, and pulled herself up.

William jumped out of the car and hurried toward her. He glanced to his sides, wary of prying eyes. The neighborhood was still.

"What are you doing?" he asked.

"I believe this house will have a pool."

"What? Why the hell do you want a pool?" William scanned the world around him again. It was still all clear. "Fay, this is breaking and entering. You go to jail for this."

Fay dropped down on the other side, where she landed gracefully. The hours at the strip club had clearly paid off. She felt her forehead.

"Come on, William. I don't have much time. I might need your help. It feels worse than some of the previous times."

"What feels worse?"

Fay didn't reply. She ran to the backyard.

"Fay," William called after her to no response. He glanced again to both sides and then observed the home but saw no activity. "Fuck me." He climbed the gate.

It wasn't as easy to get over as Fay made it appear. Once he got to the other side, he sprinted to the backyard, hoping to find her before they broke any more laws. Fay was becoming more trouble than she was worth. If only he'd gone with the cousin of one of his friends. What was her name? Molly or Holly? He couldn't remember. Sure, she was a bit of a nerd and not his type appearance wise, but at least he'd be at the prom and not perpetrating a crime.

Rounding the wall to the backyard, he heard a splash.

Fay stood in the center of a pool, screaming and flapping her arms around like a kid in the ocean. The house lights were all off. He hoped that whoever owned the place stayed away for the night. Fay screamed again, but it wasn't a cry of joy. She was in pain.

"What's going on?" he asked, reaching the pool's edge.

She swam to him. "I'm burning up. It usually goes away. But it's not working this time. I can't understand it."

"What are you talking about?"

Fay opened her mouth to speak, but instead of words, a puff of gray smoke came out. She stretched for the edge of the pool. William had to bend down and grab her hands, which felt hot.

"Are you okay?" he asked, but she didn't reply. He pulled her to the pool's steps.

William released her burning hands. Fay, on all fours on the top step, lifted her head. Her eyes were pitch black, like holes the color of the darkest spots in the nighttime sky. William stepped back, noticing her hair stood up, except it wasn't hair. Yellow, orange, and red flames blazed atop her head.

"What's going on?"

Fay's skin glowed red. The dress she wore burst into flames, burning until reduced to ashes that fluttered around her like charcoal butterflies. She opened her mouth and fire came roaring out, sending William ducking. He escaped the flames, but the fire engulfed a plastic chair near the pool. It started to drip, melting before his eyes.

Fay dunked her head under the water. Bubbles popped at the surface, like boiling water. William, looking around for help, decided he needed to get out of here. He could place an anonymous call to someone. Staying with whatever was going on with Fay wasn't happening.

He got up.

"Wait," Fay said.

Fay, standing on the top step, naked, waved away the smoke rising from her body. Her hair, skin, and eyes were back to normal.

"What the fuck was that all about?" William asked.

"I told you I have a condition. It was worse tonight. It's passed, though."

William's mind first told him it must have been a trick, but he knew that wasn't true. Something weird was going on with Fay. It occurred to him that he was staring at her breasts. Her pink nipples were hard; she shivered.

"Um, here you go." William took off his suit jacket and handed it to her.

"Thank you."

"I-I think you need to see a doctor about your condition. I don't really know what else to say. I'm freaked out."

"I'll be fine. We must get going. You're already late."

"What? You can't be serious after what happened."

"It's fine now. I keep a backup dress in my bag."

"I-I—"

"It's okay. Even if we only have one dance, you deserve it." Fay reached for William's hand.

He wanted to flinch, fearful it would be hot. It was warm, but a good warm. Together they walked around the pool and made their way back to the front yard, where they climbed over the gate. No police awaited them, and the house remained dark. William's relief was instant. They'd managed to get away with the strange episode in the pool.

"So what's this?" someone on William's right said.

William turned to face the person. A tall, bald man climbed from the front of a vehicle parked behind his. It was Baldy, the man he had seen with the burn scars at the club.

"What are you doing here? Did you follow us?" Fay asked.

Baldy pulled out a pistol, then aimed it at Fay's head. "You're a lying bitch. Tell me you don't go with customers. Look at you. I bet you're naked under the jacket. Don't think I don't know what you two did in that pool. I heard screaming and splashing. You're filthy animals."

"That's not what happened."

"I know what—"

A red glow erupted around Fay. She opened her mouth, and a fireball the size of a baseball, with a tail of flames behind it, came flying out. It shot toward Baldy. He ducked. The fireball, which had increased its size to that of a soccer ball, flew over him.

"Don't do that again!" Baldy pulled out a small container of pills from his pocket. "See what you turn into when you don't have these?" he said, shaking the container with one hand and aiming the gun at Fay's chest with the other. "Try the fire nonsense on me again, and I pull the trigger."

Fay clenched her fists. "You stole my medication."

"Yes, I did. Do you take me for an idiot? I wanted to be there for you. And look what happened to me."

"You attacked me onstage."

"So I had a few beers in me. Did I deserve this?"

"It was an accident. I was scared."

William had first wanted to run when he'd seen the weapon, but there was something about Fay. He couldn't leave her. He was good at communicating; maybe he could speak some sense into this guy. Hell, William would even offer him some money if it got him to leave Fay alone. Deciding it was time to take control of the situation, William walked between Baldy and Fay.

"Why don't you chill," William said, lifting his hands to show he had no weapon. "Put the gun away, and let's talk this out like—"

Baldy pulled the trigger.

A hit to the chest knocked William backward. Dizziness overwhelmed his senses, and he fell to the hard ground. A stinging warmth rose in his chest. His senses heightened, and he heard a car speed away. Someone was screaming. It was high pitched and forceful. He focused, trying to decipher who was shouting.

"Help, somebody help," Fay screamed.

"What time is it?" William muttered. For some reason, his mind told him he probably wasn't going to make it to the prom. This was surely nonsense. Yes, Baldy had shot him, but the pain had ceased.

Fay bent down. "Hang on. I'm calling an ambulance."

William tried to speak again, but a bitter-tasting liquid had filled his mouth, and all he could do was make a choking sound.

His mind told him again he wouldn't make the prom.

This time, he believed it.

UNIDENTIFIED FATHERLY OBJECT

His plans hadn't come together overnight. They'd required meticulous preparation. When Fred Garcia realized Father's Day was only a week away, the perfect date for his operation had presented itself. It seemed too good to be true. For a moment, as he sat in the living room of his uncle and aunt's home, positive energy flowed through him. It had been over a year since his father's accident, and Fred now had his mission.

He took a sip of coffee.

Nothing on the TV interested him. The map in front of him did. He had circled red areas of interest thanks to information he'd collected from the Internet. Knowing where to search would be critical if he was to find any evidence. Yes, he had read the press release that the military gave the media. It wasn't good enough. Cold, hard proof was all that would allow him to continue with his life.

"What do you have there?" his aunt, Maria, asked from behind him.

Fred folded the map and looked back to her. Transfixed by his mission, he hadn't heard his aunt and uncle arrive home. "How was dinner?"

"Don't avoid my question." Maria placed her handbag on the wooden table near her. "Now answer me," she said, walking toward Fred.

"It's nothing."

"Nothing? How many times have we told you to stop this nonsense? I'm sorry about what happened to your father, but going onto military property is out of the question. These delusions need to stop."

Fred stood. "Don't you care what really happened?"

"I know what happened. The military released a statement. They even paid for the wonderful funeral. It was a tragedy, Fred. But your father always knew the risks."

Fred clenched his fists. The story of what happened sounded like a plot to a bad science-fiction movie. His father, a scientist, had occasionally helped the military with classified projects. It was work his father never spoke of, which seemed odd, as his father used to love talking to him about the things he did, even the classified type. Fred knew it wasn't the kind of project his father wanted to do, but the money was too good to turn down. The cash would have allowed his father to pursue other projects that truly inspired him.

Maria sighed, pulling Fred from his thoughts. "You have to move on with your life," she said, looking toward the hallway, no doubt seeking Fred's uncle, Tony, to back her up.

Fred didn't wait.

He gripped the map at his side and walked past his aunt. Heading straight for his room, he heard his uncle say, "What's it now?" to his aunt's moans.

"He's going to trespass on the military base again," Maria said.

"He'll get over it," Tony said. "Give him some time."

Fred closed his bedroom door. He wouldn't get over it. His operations were well past the point of return. On Father's Day, he was going to sneak into the military base outside of town and find out what happened to his dad.

* * *

Fred opened one of the store's fridges. A cabbage smell filled his nostrils, and the fridge was cool, not cold. He took out an energy drink regardless. In his other hand, he held his phone. He had already logged the coordinates he intended to inspect into his GPS. He'd noted the weakest spots around the base after some exploratory missions near the large fence protecting the perimeter. Everything appeared old and reasonably unprotected, almost as if the military wanted to give off the illusion that the base was nothing more than some run-down operation collecting dust. Fred knew better. His father had let slip that one of the warehouses at the base contained state-of-the-art equipment.

High-pitched laughter crackled from the front of the store. Fred made his way down the aisle, his sneakers squeaking on the linoleum. A man stood at the counter, his arms outstretched as if indicating that he had caught a monster-sized fish.

"Now, I never said aliens. All I told you was I saw some weird lights the other night," the tall man, wearing a beige hunting jacket over a black shirt, said. He dropped his arms to his sides.

"What's so special about lights?" the shop assistant asked. "When you said 'strange activity,' I thought you were going to reveal something juicy."

"Lights at a military station meant to be abandoned for over a year? That seems juicy to me. It's not the first time either. Now I'm not saying it's a UFO cover-up or anything like the Area 51 stuff, but it's strange to see so much movement there. I've driven past many nights before, and I haven't seen anything other than darkness. The last two weeks, however, I've seen lights every night. Something is definitely going on."

Fred stopped before exiting the aisle. He didn't want the two men to see him and cease their conversation. Any info on the old base—even if it wasn't completely trustworthy—could be gold. He crouched, careful not to make any noise, and leaned in.

The shop assistant tapped the counter. "Maybe they're finally clearing the place out. I heard the rumors that there were bomb blasts and other nonsense going off there last year."

"Yeah? But why would they clear out the place at night? If it's so abandoned, they could just as well do it during the day." The man took a cigarette from the pack he had purchased. "Cool if I light one?"

"Go ahead. So, what you think they're up to?"

"Maybe they're trying to get the place running again, or storing weapons. Hell, maybe they're—"

"Hey!" the shop assistant shouted. "What are you doing over there?"

Fred stood. The assistant must have seen him on one of the shop's many security cameras. "Nothing. I was looking for something."

"What? What're you looking for?"

"Ah, nothing. It's fine," Fred said, strolling to the counter.

It was as he had feared. Both men went dead quiet about the base as he paid for his drink. He refused to give in and decided to wait outside.

It didn't take long for the other customer to emerge from the bright, artificial lights of the store. The man flicked away his cigarette end and headed toward a blue pickup.

Fred walked after him. "Excuse me."

The man turned around and narrowed his eyes at Fred. "What you want?"

"I'm sorry. But I overheard you in there talking about the old military base. I was curious where you saw the lights."

The man grinned. He scratched the side of his face. "Yeah, I saw the lights. Why do you want to know?"

"Seriously, I'm just curious. I've seen the old base and often wondered what used to go down over there."

"You don't plan on wandering around there? You'd only get yourself shot."

"No, not at all." Fred stuck out his hand. "I'm Fred."

The man shook his hand. "Marty Jenkins."

Marty took another cigarette out and lit it. He puffed smoke into the night sky. "Well, Fred. Curiosity will cost you. Twenty dollars, and I'll tell you exactly where I saw the lights."

"I only have ten and some change."

Marty frowned. "That'll do."

* * *

Fred knew exactly where Marty had seen the lights. The old abandoned tank covered in dust was within sight of the fence during the day. He'd even marked it on his map. He parked his car on the side of the road, behind a large bush. It didn't hide much of the vehicle, but it was nighttime and any cover would do. Shining his flashlight onto the map, he nodded. He was close enough to proceed on foot.

Moving along the perimeter of the fence, he was careful about when to switch his flashlight on. Fortunately, the moon and stars above provided Fred with enough illumination to traverse the dark, desert-like world without tripping over large stones or other obstacles. Checking his phone's dimmed screen, he stopped when he confirmed that he should be near the area of the tank. He shined his flashlight around the base, but the beam didn't reach far enough. Fred cursed and stomped his foot. He allowed himself a moment to regain equilibrium. Scanning the fence, he caught the "Warning: Electric Fence" sign. Fred knew better, however; he had tested the fence before.

He reached out; the tips of his fingers met the fence.

There was no shock.

He searched his backpack for the cutters he had taken from his uncle's garage and got to work on the fence. Once he'd made a hole big enough, he crawled through without hindrance. Being short and skinny had some advantages after all. The anxiety reached new levels as his feet touched military ground, and Fred inhaled deep breaths, trying to calm his heartbeat and the cold sweat taking over the surface of his body. Thoughts of his father helped stem the tide, and he stood, expecting the worst.

There was no alarm, no spotlight shining at him. No soldiers rushed to his position. Silence reigned.

Fred moved forward, keeping low. He needed to find the old tank. Marty had said that if you were facing the tank from the perimeter and walked toward it, and then went twenty-five degrees to its right, you'd head straight for the lights.

The tank didn't reveal itself.

After fifteen minutes of searching, Fred considered surrendering the current plan. He could either call it quits for the night, or go back to his vehicle and try targeting one of the other locations he had marked on the map.

As he stared at the dark landscape ahead of him one last time, more in desperation than with the expectation of seeing anything, something did appear in his view. It wasn't any type of military vehicle, and it was a good distance from him, but it was large, much larger than a tank. His right foot stepped forward before his brain had even decided to inspect the shape in the night.

Continuing his journey into the darkness, Fred noticed that the shape was a warehouse. It didn't sit clustered with the other buildings on his map, which were all situated on another part of the base. It stood alone. He had to extinguish another flame of thought. There were times when he imagined coming out to the base and uncovering the truth behind what happened to his father. There were also the few times where he couldn't resist dreaming of running into his father. The military may have lied. He'd never seen a body, as they said the remains in the casket were unrecognizable. That was no proof of his father's demise. Regardless, Fred knew such hopes set him up for disappointment. It was best to take the operation one small step at a time.

A light came on at the warehouse. It illuminated a door below, a door only a stone's throw away from Fred.

The door opened.

Fred dived onto the ground. He feared capture, but there was nothing he could do but hope whoever came out wouldn't look in his direction.

A figure appeared, wearing military gear and what looked like some type of mask. Possibilities ran wild in Fred's mind: night-vision goggles? A gas mask? He ceased the thoughts. The soldier didn't look at him, nor did he head in Fred's direction. Instead, he walked away, disappearing into the night.

Fred, trying to keep as low as possible, moved toward the door. He paused before it. There were no markings or numbers. He saw no camera or keypad, no security devices of any kind. There was only a bronze door handle.

Fred reached for it.

The handle turned, unlocked.

It all seemed too easy. Even if the base was in the process of abandonment, surely they'd still lock the doors. Fred had come past the point of no return, however. He opened the door to darkness. He expected to take a step inside and feel for a light switch on the wall near him, except as he took the first step into the warehouse, the lights switched on automatically.

Illumination from harsh fluorescent bulbs rained down on him. He stood in a large room about half the size of the warehouse. PC screens and other electronic equipment sat on desks lining the walls. A large board to his right drew his attention.

Fred ran his hand over some of the pictures and articles. The images and stories were like something you'd expect to see in a conspiracy theorist's trailer. He read a few of the headlines. There were mentions of a girl seeing a ghost eat her boyfriend at a festival in

China, a guy that claimed vampires attacked him in an abandoned warehouse, and a zombie outbreak on a beach in Mexico. Fred ignored the chill that ran down his spine. There was another article about parents claiming little devil creatures had possessed their kids. Others described peculiar events of rituals where victims were drowned and of a woman who could turn into fire. Fred took a step back, needing a break from the board.

A *ping* sound alerted him to activity behind him.

There was another door.

Fred walked to it, eager to document all the strange things he was seeing. Time was his enemy. The soldier could return at any moment. He would have a look in the next room and then begin taking photos. There was a saying about curiosity, but he couldn't recall it. His palms were sweaty as he reached for the door handle.

Unlocked.

The next room was similar in size to the first, but it had large steel tables in its center. Medical equipment filled the spaces along the walls. Fortunately, there were no bodies, alien or human. The space was also incredibly clean. A strong medicinal aroma hung in the air, and it burned Fred's nostrils. An object stood out on one of the tables to the far right. It looked like a large snow globe.

Something rested inside it.

The object in the globe reminded Fred of the bizarre specimens or organs kept in jars of formaldehyde that he had seen in horror movies. He ran his fingers over the cold table as he rounded it. There was definitely some type of creature in the globe, but no liquid or substance preserved it. No, it wasn't a creature. Fred's body iced from the feet up as his brain processed the information transmitted from the optic nerve.

His father's head was in the globe.

The eyes looked straight at him.

* * *

"Fred?"

The voice sounded tinny, but there was no mistaking it. Fred stepped back and bumped into a table behind him. A jar fell over, threatening to roll off the table. Fred didn't stop it. He turned back to the head of his father.

"Fred?"

It wasn't possible. How could a head talk? Where was his body?

"Fred. What are you doing here?"

The world shook like jelly on a plate. Fred reached back and used the table to support himself, feeling faint. Nausea rocked him, and he shut his eyes, holding tight as his world wobbled off course. Surely, when he opened his eyes, the head would be gone.

It wasn't.

"Fred. I'm talking to you. You shouldn't be here. How did you find me?"

"I—"

"You need to leave, son. This is not the place to be. You can't be seen here with what's going on."

"Leave?" Anger spewed up from Fred's gut like erupting lava. "What's going on? Why—why are you in that thing? What happened?"

"They're running this base and trying to help us. We left this area for a while after some accidents, but we returned once we figured things had died down. There's something coming, son. You have to understand that I and others had to do this to try and protect the world."

"What are you talking about?"

"Weird things have been happening all round the globe. These events are leading up to one final attack. It will be the end of life as we know it. Once we figured out how to communicate with each other, they showed us the signs of danger. It's something even they fear. They've come to try and help us, as it will target them eventually."

Fred shook his head. He had never used drugs harder than marijuana at the odd party, but he was beginning to wonder if this was what it felt like to be high on something more potent. Was he poisoned? Was something he'd touched laced with a chemical? There had to be another explanation for what he saw.

"Now, son. I need you to get out of here. Trust that I worked here for the right reasons."

"Shut up," Fred shouted. "I don't know what you're talking about. Where is your body? What happened to you?"

"Please don't shout. I can't protect you if they come. They have authority in this base to do what they need."

It was his father, but it wasn't. It was impossible, but it was real. There was also something off about how his father spoke, almost as if he didn't have full comprehension. Why did he babble such madness?

Tears streaked Fred's cheeks. "What happened, Dad? Did you get hurt?"

"We were testing something to hopefully combat the enemy, but it failed. I was gravely injured. They had a way to keep me alive—well, at least my head. They need my expertise. I'm sorry you must see me this way, but I had to help complete the work we'd started. The military said they'd provide for you and the family."

"I don't care about their money." Fred slammed his hand against his thigh. "They did this to you. They shouldn't have gotten you involved."

"Behind you, Fred. Run."

"What?" Fred said. His father's voice still sounded tinny, but higher-pitched. Seeing his father caused different emotions to entangle in his gut. He needed to do something, but he wasn't sure what. This was one possibility he hadn't prepared for.

"Please don't hurt him," his father said.

"Who are you talking to?" Fred asked, turning around.

Two soldiers stood behind him, covered by shadows from a large screen attached to one of the walls. It wasn't possible. He would have seen or heard their entry. Maybe the shock had numbed his senses. Anger rose within him, shattering the ceiling in his mind. These men did this to his father. They had to pay.

Fred dug into his backpack and pulled out his uncle's firearm, which he'd liberated before leaving home. He aimed the weapon at the two men.

One of them stepped forward. His face came into the light, but there was something wrong about it. It reminded Fred of the soldier he'd seen leave the building. He had thought it could have been a mask then, but now—now he knew better.

They weren't human.

It may have appeared as if they had limbs like people, with the long-sleeved shirts and pants covering their true appearance. Nothing hid their faces. The pale gray skin and large, oval black eyes sent chills over Fred's shoulders. He stepped back, praying his brain would find some course of action other than panic.

The soldier—no—the alien stepped toward him.

Fred pulled the trigger.

The bullet hit the alien in the upper right chest, causing it to flinch back. Fred darted for his father while dispensing bullets at the aliens. He was unsure if any hit, but he focused now on getting out with his dad, who he lifted from the table and tossed into his backpack. He ignored the tinny voice pleading with him to stop.

Fred shut the first door behind him, and then moved one of the desks before the door. The aliens didn't come bursting through as he expected. Maybe the shots had wounded them, but they never once screamed while he fired.

When he hit the cool outside air, he almost toppled over. He reached for a spot on his chest that was heating up. A warm, sticky substance met his fingers. Whatever it was, it wasn't good. He figured it must be some residue, like blood, that had splattered onto him when he'd shot at the aliens. The substance had burned through his jacket, and Fred ripped his top off before the foreign goo could do any more damage.

He took another step. His leg wobbled but didn't buckle.

His vehicle seemed so far away.

Home seemed even farther.

* * *

Fred opened his eyes to a white ceiling. Realizing he lay in his bed, the hope of it all being some bad dream surfaced. He ran his hand over his bare stomach, knowing it had all been real.

He'd made it home, barely.

Fred scanned the room, but he didn't see his backpack. Panic gripped his chest like the talons of a gigantic bird. His mind attempted to go back in time to replay his arrival home. Fragmented images were first to come forward, but a solid memory broke through. He had left the bag on the desk in his room before he'd collapsed onto his bed. More memories intruded, and he recalled his aunt and uncle were spending the night at one of their kids' homes for Father's Day. He dismissed any more thoughts.

"Dad?"

He got no response.

There was no bag on his desk.

Fred opened his bedroom door and exited into the hallway. He had to find his backpack. He needed to find his father.

A small aluminum ladder stood right before him, and a red flag popped up in the fore of Fred's mind. He couldn't remember it being there when he had come home, but disorientation had clouded his being back then. Was it the shock? Or was it the strange goo that had affected him? He looked at his wristwatch, hoping to calculate how much time had passed since he'd first left on his mission, but the hand had stopped. His watch must have broken during the drama in the warehouse.

Fred took a few heavy steps toward the ladder, reminding himself of a caveman trying to walk after reanimation from an icy slumber.

Nothing peculiar stood out about the ladder, yet Fred wondered why it would be here in the first place and how he missed it. He glanced up instinctively and saw a soccer-ball-sized hole directly above him. The hole led into the attic, and its blackness stood out against the white ceiling. His brain kicked into gear, and he concluded that his uncle must have begun the process of putting in a new light fixture.

He must have missed it when he came home.

Fred stepped forward, aiming to go around the ladder, but he heard a click. He looked up. The attic light was on.

"Uncle Tony, are you up there?" Fred asked. It seemed the most likely scenario.

"Can't we leave?"

It was the tinny voice of his father, but how had he gotten into the attic?

"Dad?"

"Don't—"

"Dad?" Fred said again. The tinny voice was gone, leaving him in the silence of the house. Frustrated and with the slightest spark of fear building within him, Fred gripped the ladder and placed his foot on the first rung. For a moment, he considered using the retractable attic ladder, but his uncle had an affinity for locking things. There wasn't time to search for the key. He shook his head, sighed, and then nodded when he reaffirmed to himself that he only wanted a peek.

Fred ascended the ladder.

When he placed his feet on the penultimate rung, the top of his head was inches from the hole. He turned his neck side to side, trying to see if anything stood near the hole—nothing did. "Dad, are you up there?"

No reply.

Tightening his hold on the ladder, he braced through a wave of unsteadiness. Summoning courage, he placed his right foot onto the last rung and raised his head into the hole, slowly, safely. The sides brushed against his ears. The hole was just big enough for his head to pass through.

He saw nothing.

His uncle had cleaned out the attic months ago. There was nowhere to hide. Yet something was off. His view seemed dull, and he couldn't bring an arm through, so he moved his head forward until he hit something. He repeated this action all around him. It appeared to be some kind of plastic bubble.

Fred had endured enough; he needed to search the rest of the house for his father before deciding what to do about what he'd seen at the warehouse. His father's voice may have come from somewhere else in the home, and peculiar acoustics had simply deceived him. As he attempted to move his head down, something tightened around the middle of his neck. His head couldn't exit the attic. He couldn't get back down. His heart thundered, but he fought for lucid thought. Two figures, blurry at first, walked into his field of vision. They became clearer as he focused.

It was them.

The two aliens had found him.

He could take no more and screamed. His voice failed to escape the odd contraption around his head. Drawing breath, he found the air thin and barely sufficient. The shorter of the two aliens gestured to the taller one. The taller alien reached out. There was some black remote-like device in his hand. A click went off in the bubble around Fred's head, and something cold spiked into the back of his neck.

Fred attempted to rotate his head, but to no avail. Sharp, warm tingling exploded all around the back of his skull. The peculiar feeling faded, replaced by numbness. A crackle tickled his ears, and then a faint hum surrounded him inside the globe. He wanted to flap his arms and kick out with his legs in the hope he would go crashing back down, but for some reason he couldn't will movement. The contraption must have injected him with some type of poison, causing paralysis.

The two aliens each took a step closer, as they fiddled with devices alongside their necks. There was a hiss of gas that shimmered green before it vanished into the air. The taller alien appeared to be removing his face. Fred prayed they were humans with impressive masks, pulling a disturbing and elaborate prank on him. Reality wasn't so kind. They weren't human, and apart from having limbs resembling arms and legs, they didn't look anything like the aliens in films. No doubt, these mainstream alien-looking helmets or masks, with the black eyes and gray skin, were designed to mislead humans and hide their true identities. Seeing their real faces caused Fred's brain to shudder.

To say they looked similar to the heads of slugs or snails would be doing all *Gastropoda*-class species an injustice. These beings were a special kind of ugly. Their faces glowed purple and had strange outbreaks of some gray fungus. Their oval eyes, bulging out of shortened eyestalks, were white marble in color, and each eye had a ring of red dots in the center. Three black slits sat where a mouth would have been, and a mustard-yellow froth foamed at the sides of the slits. Fred could bear the scene no longer and gagged as another wave of dizziness hit him.

Fred heard what sounded like the squeaking of a pack of rats. He assumed that this was some type of communication.

"What have you done?" Fred shouted. There was a crackle, almost like static, in the contraption. His voice sounded like the robots in old science-fiction films. He wanted to cry, but no tears formed. The horrific realization that they had trapped him in something like a snow globe, a mere trinket of curiosity for these otherworldly beings, infuriated and frightened him.

"You won't get away with this."

When he still got no response, he proceeded to launch into a barrage of obscenities. The alien holding the remote must have understood that what he said wasn't flattering. It pressed something on the remote, which sent a spike of current through Fred's head. His thoughts, his consciousness, froze as if dipped into Arctic waters.

Fred watched in silence as they put their masks—or helmets—back on. Had they only revealed their identity to increase the dread that pumped within him?

"Please, just let me go and give me back my father," Fred said as some ability returned to his brain.

The tall alien shook its head and pressed the button on the remote. Once more the current flooded Fred's brain.

As his mind fought through the fog, he realized they had set up the ladder and made the hole all for catching him. Was it a sick game, or maybe a form of punishment for him shooting at them? It would have been simpler to kill him in his room. If there had been any truth to his father telling him they were here to help humanity, it was clearly on their own terms.

The taller alien curled one of its hands around the ball Fred was in. Fred tried to move, to do anything, but he still couldn't shake the feeling of paralysis.

The alien lifted him up and turned him upside down. Fred managed to glance back down the hole he had stuck his head through. There it was... The cold, hard truth hit him in the face like a boxer landing a jaw-shuddering blow.

He had been decapitated.

His body had fallen back into the passage, knocking over the ladder. A pool of his blood now stained his aunt's rug. Like his father, all that remained of him was his head. Fred assumed the strange globe containing him preserved his brain and its operations—at least to some degree. He did feel a lag in his mind's capabilities. It appeared to be the same problem that affected his father. A sudden rush of conflicting emotions—hysteria, sadness, and fear—stirred within him.

There would be no waking from this nightmare.

The truth of what had happened to his father and what was going on in the military warehouse would never surface. He'd failed and was now nothing more than a paperweight for beings from another world.

Fred did the only thing that came to mind.

He screamed.

INDEPENDENCE DENIED

A siren whined, ripping Brad Marshall from his nap on the sofa. He checked the time on his wristwatch, realizing he had fallen asleep for nearly an hour since arriving home from work. His stomach groaned, but Brad didn't want to get up and make something to eat just yet. His job had been draining the last few weeks, but in three days, on the fourth of July—or Independence Day, as his uncle kept reminding him— he was taking a few days off to see some family. The open beer on the coffee table seemed a suitable alternative to having to make dinner, at least for the moment. Taking a sip, he felt something in his mouth, something in the warm, bitter liquid that shouldn't be there.

He spat out the beer.

A bug had decided to drown itself while he'd been asleep.

"Nasty." Brad wiped his mouth.

Sirens boomed from the TV in front of him. Brad read the white font in the red box at the bottom of the screen. "Breaking news: Tsunami hits the coast of Thailand. Thousands feared dead."

Brad shook his head. He didn't have any interest in bad news and switched to a new channel, only to find someone reporting on the disaster there as well.

Something was different. Brad increased the volume. The female reporter with curly brown hair said that an earthquake had hit San Francisco.

Two massive natural disasters were happening at the same time. Relieved he stayed in Florida, Brad flicked through the channels, curious to see what other news stations showed. As expected, they all reported on the disasters. An expert in climatology spoke on one of the channels. The bald man in the charcoal suit raged about climate change and how nature struck back at humanity.

Brad hit the mute button. His stomach groaned, and he stood. Would the disasters affect the active research at his work?

As he grabbed a cold slice of yesterday's pizza, his mind drifted to whether he should watch a movie or play a game on his computer. Whatever choice he made, it wouldn't take long for thoughts of work the next morning to disappear altogether.

* * *

Nobody paid much attention when Brad walked into work nearly twenty minutes late. Everyone in the office was either huddled around a screen or hovering in groups, deep in conversation.

Brad entered the professor's office, where his first job was always to turn all the computers and other equipment on. Today, however, the PCs and any necessary equipment were already at work. Brad expected the professor to pop out from the desk in his office, but he was alone. He'd been working for

Professor Masterson for nearly a year. It wasn't too bad, except for when the professor expected him to find anomalies in some of the research. Brad much preferred monitoring the screens on another desk to his right.

He sat at the desk, adjusting the front of the lucky red baseball cap he wore. The center screen had a tag that read "Main Visual" above it, while the screen on the left read "Data" and the one on the right "Map." The data was boring, with its perpetual flow of numbers and words. The map showed a blinking red dot in its center.

"Where are you going, Mandy?" Brad asked, scratching his head.

He looked to the visual screen.

A month ago, off the coast of Florida, Professor Masterson and a team of marine biologists had attached a digital camera to Mandy's fin. She was a great white shark, and instead of staying near the coast—usual behavior for her this time of year based on data gathered from other experts—she had headed deeper into the ocean, which set off the map's alert. Watching the visual brought a sense of wonder. Brad hadn't been that excited to stare at the screen of the ocean when first hired, but as he'd learned more about the realm and its creatures, it had attracted him evermore. He saw what Mandy saw as she journeyed into the ocean depths. It was usually nothing more than empty spaces of dark water, but on occasion she'd pass other animals, and the best was when she fed.

Shapes burst to life before him, almost as if the screen had heard his thoughts about hoping for some action.

"What's going on?" Brad said, leaning closer.

A plethora of sea animals circled a mass of whitish water that reminded Brad of a vortex, only less powerful. Along with Mandy, he saw other great whites, hammerhead sharks, blacktips, dolphins, whales, and even seals. The vortex's power waned, and an image at its center cleared. Brad's nose almost touched the screen as the visual lured him in. He moved back to get a better overall picture and gasped. An anthropoid-like behemoth with near-human arms and legs filled his view. Its strange head—if it was a head—chilled the blood in Brad's veins. It resembled an octopus, and a mass of tentacles emanated from where a mouth would be. Brad even thought he saw wings attached to the creature's back, but the underwater lighting may have created the effect.

"What's going on?" Brad asked himself.

The door behind him clicked open. He spun around, expecting to see the professor.

"Hi, Brad," Delilah Love said, adjusting her black-rimmed glasses sitting askew on her nose. She'd tied up her platinum-blonde hair, which had light purple streaks at the ends, and wore a pink sweater too big for her small frame. This was her usual look. Delilah was another assistant in the office, though she worked with a different leader on the team. "I saw you come in, and I wanted to bring you a coffee."

"Um, yes." Brad wanted to scold her for entering the office without knocking, even if it wasn't technically his office. He decided not to because he didn't want to do something suspicious that could attract her attention to the visuals of the ocean. A peculiar excitement within kept him from wanting to share his discovery yet. Instead, he flicked the visual screen's Off switch, knocking over a container of pens as he did so.

"What was that?" Delilah asked.

"What was what?" Brad looked back at the screen. It was off.

"I saw a film or something. You're meant to be working."

"Delilah, you should really mind your own business. Good grief. Please just put the coffee down and go. And knock first next time."

"I was kidding, Brad." Delilah tapped Brad's shoulder. "Anyway, I sometimes play games on the PC when I should be working. Don't tell Maggie."

"Yes, yes, just—"

The ground beneath them shook violently, as if the Devil and his horde of minions were trying to drill their way up. Folders, framed photographs, and other items fell to the office floor. Brad gripped the desk; Delilah clung onto his shoulders, her nails digging into him.

Time slowed. The rumbling continued for what felt an eternity, but Brad knew it'd only lasted one well-held-in breath. He exhaled, canceling the idea to duck under the desk as the world around him found its usual calm.

"Oh my God," Delilah said, releasing his shoulders. "That was an earthquake. And right here, by us."

"Yeah."

"I hope no one is hurt."

Brad didn't care about the earthquake. Sure, he had gotten a fright, and seismic activity was interesting on some level, but he wanted to return to the image of the behemoth in the ocean. He ushered Delilah out of the office, telling her he wanted to clean up and that she should check on all the other staff. His real intentions, however, were to check on the screen and download Mandy's footage of the creature before the professor arrived.

He switched on the visual screen.

Mandy was back to swimming through dark, empty waters.

Brad knew better.

* * *

Brad threw one of his shoes across the living room. He had rushed home after work, having managed to download the strange recordings. Fortunately, Professor Masterson didn't show for work; the government had summoned him to a special meeting. Not everything was going Brad's way. Playing the footage on his TV screen proved futile. He couldn't locate the creature. It didn't help that Delilah had rattled him, and thus he didn't recall exactly what time he'd seen it.

Brad stood. He walked around the sofa, taking the opportunity to curse at the TV every now and again.

"I know I saw it. I know I'm not going mad," he said. "I'll watch the whole thing from the beginning if I have to."

Brad fell back onto his sofa. He reached for his remote and accidentally changed the channel. Choice swearwords appeared in the fore of his mind, but he ceased those thoughts as the words "Breaking News: Third Earthquake Reported" scrolled across the bottom of the TV in black font with a yellow background.

"Ah, the damn earthquake," Brad mumbled, recalling how everyone had made such a fuss over the event at work.

It wasn't the seismic event he'd thought of. The reporter did mention the one Brad had experienced, but there had been two more. One had occurred in Warsaw, Poland, and another in Buenos Aires, Argentina. She also mentioned a tornado and a volcanic eruption.

"Three earthquakes, a tornado, and a volcanic eruption," Brad said, contemplating if he should fetch a beer. "That's a bit odd."

"Leading seismologists are baffled and fear more activity," the news reporter said. "Over a thousand people have been estimated to have been killed in the three quakes and other disasters. The cost of damage to buildings and infrastructure is in the billions." She went on to say that this, added to the tsunami and earthquake from the previous evening, had led to a special meeting between some of the world's leading scientists. They still had no answers as to what was happening. The reporter then went through areas that might come under threat from any further natural disasters.

The news sparked his curiosity, but it wasn't the behemoth in the ocean. Brad flicked the channel back to the footage from this morning. He wouldn't be able to relax until he saw it again. He needed to know what it was.

Brad watched from the beginning, but all he saw was dark water. He sat up and leaned forward on the sofa, focusing. He'd pause when any shape or change in lighting appeared on the screen.

The creature didn't appear.

"You've got to be kidding me," Brad shouted when he came to the end of the footage again. He stood, wanting to throw the remote at the screen, but he resisted the urge burning his core like fire. "This can't be happening."

He needed a release and kicked at the coffee table in front of him. His foot missed one of the legs—his intended target—and lifted the glass top instead. The glass moved off its frame and shattered on the ground, causing Brad to hold his hands up as he cursed the gods above.

It didn't make sense.

Brad rushed toward the fridge. He retrieved some beers, but they wouldn't be potent enough, so he took out a bottle of whiskey from one of the top cupboards. After returning to the living room, he pressed Play on the footage, starting from the beginning again.

He opened the whiskey and took a swig.

Brad had no intentions of doing anything else until he saw the creature.

* * *

Opening his eyes, Brad knew something was off. His view appeared distorted, murky, and he battled to make out his surroundings. When he stretched out with his arms, the frigid truth hit him like a sharp blade to the chest. He was underwater. Finding light in one direction, Brad swam with all his might. He surfaced, only to see a massive dark blue wave headed straight for him. It crashed over him, sending him below once again. Deeper and deeper he went as his mind tried to formulate a plan. The idea of some freak tsunami hitting the coast while he'd slept on the sofa didn't help his descent into pandemonium.

Brad stopped moving. He was floating in the ocean depths. It occurred to him he could breathe. How was that possible?

A behemoth rose from the depths less than a hundred yards from him. Its size was incredible; the sheer magnitude of this creature sent chills down Brad's spine. It looked exactly like the creature he had seen on the recording, except there were no sea animals surrounding it. Here, Brad was alone with it.

He heard words echoing in his mind, but he couldn't understand the language, and his head throbbed due to the power of the sonorous voice. He wanted to shout at the ominous monster of the deep and tell it not to say anything else, for he feared his head would explode if it did, but Brad found that he couldn't speak. Visions of destruction exploded in the fore of his mind. There were images of great cities in ruins, bodies piling up on the streets, and the sky turning gray from hungry fires eating the land.

Brad couldn't take any more. He shut his eyes, hoping that would stop the images he bore witness to, and the hurt, which now felt like someone hammering a metal spike into his brain with a sledgehammer.

As the pain reached its apex, it ceased, as if it had never been there. The images, however, remained in the back of his mind.

Brad's body rose to the surface.

The behemoth had disappeared.

* * *

A loud sound rattled Brad's head. He opened his eyes, realizing the trip beneath the ocean waves had been a nightmare after all. He rubbed his forehead, which was damp from perspiration. Trying to collect himself, he discovered the rest of his body drenched with sweat.

The doorbell rang.

"Who the hell is that?" Brad mumbled.

Approaching the front door, Brad caught sight of someone sliding something under. He didn't stop. Instead he upped his pace, unlocked the front door, and swung it open. Nobody was visible in the bright sunlight, however.

He couldn't believe it was already morning.

Shaking his head, he picked up a piece of paper. It had something written on it. He checked around to make sure he couldn't see anyone and closed the front door, deciding to make his way back to the sofa. En route he inspected the note, which read "Silverfield dock. The green warehouse. 189L."

Brad placed his feet on the wooden rim of the coffee table. Fatigue crept over him. The night's rest hadn't been peaceful or sufficient. As he tried to think who could be responsible for the odd message, his eyes grew heavy. He remembered the behemoth in the sea and how it had disappeared from the recording from the previous day. Still his eyes fought for some extra rest. Brad hadn't checked the time, but he felt confident that he could catch a quick nap.

As he positioned his body for better sleep, his alarm went off. It echoed all around the quiet, empty home.

"Shit." Brad stood. He knew by the tone it was already the second alarm, and that he was going to be late for work.

* * *

Brad sat in front of the visual screen most of the early morning. All he wanted was to find the strange creature. He needed to confirm that he wasn't losing his mind. He hadn't had time to shave that morning and scratched at his stubble, begging Mandy to locate the behemoth again. All he saw was the odd shark, whale, or other usual sea-dwelling creature. The note he knew was real, because every now and again he would glance down into his shirt pocket and see it sitting there.

A knock at the door pulled him from his thoughts.

"Come in," he said.

Delilah entered with a cup of coffee. "Maggie told me to let you know that Professor Masterson is still away. He won't be in today."

"Okay." The professor not coming in suited him fine. He would have the rest of the day to focus on his mission.

"By the way, I wanted to ask about the cap. You wear it almost every day."

Brad instinctively raised a hand to the brim of his favorite red baseball cap. "It's lucky." He could've told her it was the last gift his father had given him before passing from a heart attack, but he didn't.

"That's great. With everything going on, we could all use some luck." Delilah smiled. The action was warm, lasting longer than what felt usual for a friendly smile, but the observation was ephemeral in Brad's mind.

After Delilah left, the most interesting thing about the morning was his colleagues at work going on about earthquakes; apparently, another four had occurred in various parts of the world, from Istanbul, Turkey to Nairobi, Kenya. The world was in a state of chaos as governments and scientists tried to figure out what was going on.

After lunch, Brad took the note out of his pocket. If he couldn't spot the creature on the footage, at least he had something else to occupy his mind. He knew where the docks were, but "the green warehouse" was vague. Maybe the code wasn't a location, but rather a password of some type. The intrigue hit the right spot in his brain. He decided he would head to the docks straight after work.

Switching between the main visual screen and the time, Brad counted down to the end of the workday.

* * *

It didn't take Brad long to find the warehouse. It was almost as if the place pulled him to it, and as he stood before its small white door, which had the code "189L" spray-painted over its surface, he couldn't resist holding his hand out. Brad gripped the handle and turned it.

The door opened.

Brad entered, hearing the hustle and bustle of activity. It was no abandoned warehouse. Looking around, he saw groups of people standing about, some sitting, and even a few lying on makeshift beds on the floor. They all stopped whatever they were doing and watched him enter. Beyond them was a large section with sleeping bags and mattresses on the floor. There were stacks of crates to the right and what looked like an improvised kitchen to his left. He even saw children, most playing with toys, while some read books. The crackling of a radio surfaced when there was a lull in the other noises flooding his hearing.

"Password?" a man to his right asked.

Brad turned. The tall and muscular man made him jumpy. A knot tightened within Brad's stomach. Maybe coming hadn't been the greatest idea.

"It's okay. He's with me," a soft female voice said.

Brad looked ahead.

"Ah, brother, Brad," she said.

A woman with platinum-blonde hair walked toward him. She wore a long tan coat, and her black boots made empty *thuds* as they hit the floor. Her pale-blue eyes narrowed as she neared Brad.

It was Delilah. The contrast to her usual work look was striking, especially with her hair down and no glasses.

"We were all a bit worried about you, Brad. Well, I mean I was worried about you," she said. "Events have already progressed so far, and you've arrived in the nick of time. Another hour and we'd have locked that door. And this, my brother Brad, is the only safe place on earth."

Brad shook his head. "I'm confused. What the hell is going on? And who are these other people? Why was there a note to this place under my door? Did you put it there?"

"Some of these people are among the world's leading scientists, doctors, engineers, and others with unique skill sets deemed important for what comes next. The rest are regular, but special, people, like you and me. We are all his followers. I was one of the head recruiters for this task. Most of us have known of the final events for weeks, as you can see. I chose you to be a part of this. I like you, Brad. Plus, after I caught you seeing him, it was either bring you in or kill you. You can be my partner."

Brad frowned. "I'm losing my mind, aren't I?"

"Not at all." Delilah placed a hand on his shoulder. "You are safe now, and once the rest of the world has been cleaned up, we will start a new world, a better world. No longer will he hide, locked away. He is now free to reign."

"The creature I saw?"

"Yes. You didn't think humans would reign forever? We aren't even ants in the great scheme of things. But fear not; it's an honor to lead a new world under his rule. He speaks to us in our dreams, and he promised great things, better things."

"Wait," Brad said, rubbing his right temple. His mind was heavy, and the call for clarity itched beneath the surface of his skin. A part of him considered this was all some ruse, an act, but he couldn't understand what the goal would be. Maybe they had congregated here out of fear of the natural disaster, but why make as if there was something coming? The creature he'd seen was surely only that, some yet-undiscovered behemoth of the ocean.

"Listen, I'm not sure what's going on here, but I have to get home."

Delilah shook her head. "I'm afraid that's not possible. You see, in the next twenty-four hours there will be more earthquakes, tsunamis, and other disasters. The sea will rise, and the world as you know it will no longer exist. This is the end for the ways we have known. We must keep you here for your own good and our own. Once the twenty-four-hour period has passed, we will all go outside, and the next part of our journey will begin."

"No, I said I'm—"

Something sharp pierced Brad's right shoulder. He turned and saw a thin man wearing a white coat with a thick gray handlebar moustache standing next to him. The man had a strong musky smell. Brad looked at his arm and saw the syringe leaving his limb.

Brad mumbled, "What the?"

The world around him shuddered, his knees wobbled, and he saw a dark curtain drawing closed on either side of his view. He caught a glance of a group people. There was a young woman with curly brunette hair, and she was pale, as if she had seen a ghost. Another guy wore an eyepatch and appeared to have only one arm. Two other women seemed to be carrying weapons, as the one held what looked like an ax and the other some type of samurai sword. Was he hallucinating?

Delilah entered his field of vision before the curtain closed. "Sleep well, my brother. When you awaken, the worst shall have passed."

Brad felt her warm lips kiss his forehead.

Numbness enveloped him.

* * *

"Come on, wake up," a raspy male voice said. "It's time."

Brad opened his eyes. A man with a wild silver-gray beard stood above him. The man reeked of citrus and coffee. He appeared agitated, standing with his hands on his hips and staring down at Brad.

"What is going on?" Brad asked.

"You were out. You slept through the entire twenty-four hours of shaking. Man, I must say it got a bit hairy. But it's all over. Come on, let me get you up and outside. Everyone is already there. We don't want to miss anything."

Fighting through hazy thoughts, Brad allowed the man to help him to his feet. He glanced around, confirming that he was still in the warehouse. It was true what the old man said; there wasn't another soul in the place, barring the two of them. The contrast to the day before was worrisome. Brad tried to defuse the anger and frustration that rocked him when he realized why he had been out so long. They'd drugged him. Brad knew he had to remain calm until he could get away, or he'd risk another injection.

"Let's go," the old man said. "Come on."

Brad followed him, trying to think what the old man meant about twenty-four hours of shaking. He wondered if there'd been more earthquakes and if they had hit the US. Twenty-four hours, though? That seemed too ridiculous. It occurred to him that today was the Fourth of July. He should've been with his uncle and aunt, but here he was in a warehouse at the docks.

Outside, Brad inhaled the salty air. The people had lined up on the nearest dock, facing the ocean. Brad walked past them and gasped as he looked upon the once-scenic view to his right. Gone were the warehouses, the hotels, and the fancy homes that once gazed out on the shore. Nothing but rubble lay there now. He turned around; the warehouse was the only building still standing. Dark-gray clouds blanketed the once-blue heavens he knew, while the black smoke from many fires stretched toward the sky.

"What happened?" he asked.

"He protected us," Delilah said.

"But how?"

"He can do anything."

"I-I—"

"He's coming." Delilah passed Brad his lucky red cap. "It fell when you were injected. Sorry about that. The good doctor thought you were about to make a scene. I guess the cap was lucky after all, seeing as you're here now and most of humanity no longer is." She smiled and made her way to the front of all the people.

"Who's coming? Help?" Brad asked after her.

Delilah pointed to her left. She then faced the sea and got onto her knees. The rest of the people did the same. Brad looked to where she had pointed. The beach, far to his left, was littered with the remains of broken boats and ships. Not knowing what else to do and not wanting to cause any ripples, he fell to his knees like the rest.

"Delilah? What-what is all this?"

"You should know by now. It's the end of the world, at least the way you once knew it."

"But—"

Delilah turned around and placed her index finger over her soft red lips. She pointed with her free hand to the ocean.

Brad looked to where she pointed. A large creature broke the surface. Brad's chest contracted, and breathing became difficult. He took slow, deep breaths, and recognized the head of the beast emerging from the dark ocean.

The people around him applauded, whistled, and cheered. One even shouted, "Master has come."

These were no ordinary celebrations. The world, devoid of color, embraced a somber gray tone, and no sunlight dared to pierce the clouds overhead. A chill in the air caressed Brad's skin as he searched within for some hope that this was just a nightmare he would awaken from. Nothing but a void of despair presented itself, and still the people rejoiced.

No, these weren't ordinary celebrations.

They were dark celebrations.

242

LEPRECHAUN LUCK

The brown-haired rabbit, splayed out on the ground before him, looked as though it had come between an envious hammer and a jealous anvil. What remained of its entrails resided outside of its body, and its eyes were nowhere to be seen. A stench of wet dog and rotten fruit invaded his sense of smell. Krystal loved games, but this? This wasn't her. This was either an accident or the work of a future serial killer.

Dean Murphy backed away from the deceased creature, only for a sharp object to press against his left calf. He jolted, then turned around and was greeted by another animal that had moved on to the wilds in the sky: a deer with large light-brown antlers. This poor thing had deep slashes and cuts all over; its head was barely attached to its body.

"What the fuck," Dean muttered.

He resisted the urge to gag and examined the area for any more surprises. Fortunately, the rest of the world appeared to be normal—no more dead creatures, at least. He sighed, relieved he hadn't stumbled across some makeshift animal cemetery or possibly some deranged cult's post-ritual mess. There was probably a more logical reason for what he bore witness to.

Dean had been venturing through a wild area outside of town, filled with trees and their invasive hanging branches, when he came across the dead animals. Running after his girlfriend, Krystal, had led him to his current spot. They'd been at a bar, celebrating Saint Patrick's Day, when she'd kissed him on the cheek and whispered in his ear for him to follow her—which he had. Once outside the bar, she sprinted into the gray shadows of the evening world. Dean had followed as best he could, considering he held a jug of beer in one hand and a black plastic cauldron with some other items in the other. It didn't help that he was dressed like a leprechaun.

Dean scratched his face, where the fake red beard he wore tickled, and studied the road alongside him. Roadkill? It made perfect sense. That's all he had found, nothing more sinister. Two is a coincidence. Three is a pattern. Wasn't that a saying? He surveyed the drink in his hand. It was safe: no spillage. He sighed. Saint Patrick's Day was reserved for drinking and hanging with friends, not the current nonsense he experienced.

He sipped his beer and looked down the road. "Krystal," he shouted. "Krystal, you can come out now. I'm not spending the rest of the night searching for you. The game is over."

Where was she hiding? Behind a tree nearby, or maybe farther up the road? Dean didn't know, but he knew he wanted to get back to the festivities. He placed the black cauldron next to the road, figuring it would be safe until he returned. It contained a bag with two joints, a "spare" can of beer, a chocolate bar, and a plastic three-leaf clover—which he had enjoyed using to tickle Krystal's ear earlier that day, much to her annoyance. He downed the last of his beer and placed the jug next to the cauldron.

He reached for his smartphone and dialed.

Krystal didn't answer.

"Oh wow," Dean muttered, kicking at the road. "I guess we aren't even answering calls now." He raised his voice. "I'm heading back alone then. At least I won't be the fool wandering aimlessly as it gets darker."

Dean didn't leave. Instead, he cursed beneath his breath when he received no reaction. He started up the road, shaking his head. Krystal could be a real pain sometimes, a real pain. He reminded himself to check his sides every few steps and to also call out for her.

* * *

Dean glanced at the time on his phone and stopped. He had been walking for five minutes. There was no way Krystal would have ventured this far—not even for a game. He shook his head, realizing he must have missed her. She likely stood behind one of the trees in his wake, chuckling and high-fiving herself for fooling him. Maybe she had already gone back to town? That thought stuck, and Dean concluded she had indeed gone back to town. He decided to call her again, expecting her to answer while giggling like a child trying to hide during a game of hide-and-seek.

She didn't answer.

"Fuck this shit," he muttered and turned around.

The darkening atmosphere had a newfound chill. Either that, or the alcohol he'd consumed earlier was losing its power to warm him. He buttoned up the green leprechaun jacket he wore as sounds penetrated the world around him. He searched for where one of the sounds, a sharp crackling, had emanated from. Finding a definitive location proved difficult.

"Krystal, that you?"

The crackling sound returned; it came from behind him. As he turned around, a shadowy figure appeared in his peripheral vision. It leaped out from the tree line, almost gliding in the air. The figure landed, softly, in the middle of the road.

It wasn't Krystal.

Who was it?

More questions followed: How had they jumped? How had they landed so quietly? Why had they revealed themselves? Dean couldn't ascertain any noteworthy features other than two large red lights shining from where he expected a face to be. A costume? A mask? Both? That had to be it. This train of thought was cemented when a pair of wings shimmered under an ephemeral spell of light.

"Who are you?" Dean asked. "What do you want?"

The figure didn't respond; it didn't move at all.

"Hey, you think you're funny?"

The figure had seemingly morphed into a statue.

"You think you're going to scare me 'cause you're dressed up? That ain't happening, buddy. I don't have time for this shit."

Dean couldn't help but wish for an oncoming vehicle. That would wake this prankster up. Sadly, no car magically appeared, nor were there any lights that would even suggest one was coming. In fact, he couldn't recall seeing a vehicle since he had been in town. He shook his head and placed his hands on his hips, then lowered his gaze. It was time to get back to Krystal.

A suspicion hit with such force that he couldn't help but jerk his head back up, facing the figure. Could it be? Could it really be? This costume was too elaborate for Krystal, but maybe that explained why it had taken so long for her to show herself? She had to get as far away as possible to give herself enough time to put the over-the-top thing on.

He marched to the figure. "This ain't gonna work on me, Krystal. I'm not falling for this game. You hear me?"

The figure grunted.

There was no way the sound came from Krystal. It barely resembled any noise a human might make, but Dean banished the thought. This was likely some guy who was good at making all manner of peculiar sounds and had found an outlet for his wayward creativity. Still, Dean halted his steps. A cold sweat broke out over his body; his legs were heavy. He didn't want to take another step closer, but he didn't want to turn around and run either. The standoff was a moment that felt like an unbearable eternity.

Dean pushed his chest out, clenching his hands into fists.

The figure grunted again, this time deeper and with more force.

The newfound fear circulating within Dean aided him, sharpening his focus. If he got a sense of who he was up against, he could make a more calculated decision on how to act. The boosted processes weren't enough, for the night kept to the figure's defense, shrouding it in the darkness of mystery. Dean stepped back, now unsure if he should turn and run or look around for something to use as a weapon. He squinted, narrowing his view on the almost pixelated rendering of the unwelcome figure's visage, hoping one last time to peer through the darkness that swarmed over it. No features presented themselves from the black other than the red lights that burned brightly where eyes should sit.

"What the fuck do you want? Huh? What the fuck is your problem?"

The figure stepped forward, which briefly revealed a pallid gray countenance that sent a shiver down Dean's back. A snout-shaped structure protruded where a human nose should be, and canine-like yellow teeth lined a mouth that stretched uncannily wide. It didn't look like a mask; it didn't look human.

The creature hissed.

It stepped back, then lurched forward, sending liquid flying in Dean's direction. He didn't move in time; the warm crimson substance splattered against his face and upper body.

He needed to leave.

Dean turned around and shot off, not expecting an immediate obstacle in his way. He jumped and cleared what appeared to be another mutilated carcass. It wasn't a rabbit. It was too big. It wasn't a deer either. The pungent stench of urine and feces scorched his nostrils. As he upped his pace, the stench mercifully vacated. So, too, did the thoughts of what animal had met an early demise. Now, all that mattered was getting back to town.

A shadow moved in the skies above.

He didn't stop to look.

* * *

Dean had to stop, having burned through adrenaline like an eating-contest champion devoured hot dogs. His heart pounded in his chest. His calves ached. The world around him projected the illusion of hurtling by even though he remained still. He breathed in deep through his nostrils and exhaled slowly out his mouth, while placing his hands on his knees and leaning forward. He was out of shape, but he was still alive. Maybe wearing the leprechaun suit had brought him some luck. It was a strange thought, but he couldn't help wishing it was true. He surveyed the area, ready to run at even a microscopic hint of anything ominous.

There were no signs of the creature, neither above nor below.

The world had returned to an acceptable level of normality.

A tingling sensation erupted over his skin. Was it relief, or aftereffects from running for the first time in ages? The feeling was amplified when he saw his possessions from earlier. Both the empty jug of beer and black cauldron sat as he had left them. The tingling lost its potency, however, when he noticed the dead rabbit and deer had disappeared. He cursed, realizing the opportunity to take photos of the deceased was gone. They were all he had to give credence to his strange tale. Who would clear dead animals on the side of the road this late at night? Who would do so and leave his items untouched? Who would leave an unopened beer? A faint *screech* from behind him ended his questions.

He looked around. No sightings or sounds disturbed the world, but he couldn't shake the new idea that he was being watched. He stared at the tops of the trees nearest to him. Something about the high branches reaching into the now-nighttime sky desired his attention. The fear of being watched only grew. He forced his gaze lower, but that didn't do anything to stem the wavelike feeling of him being observed or being stalked—or worse: hunted.

"Fuck this." He grabbed his items.

The weight of the cauldron gave him pause.

He manipulated what light he could from his environment to help identify why the object weighed at least four times what he expected. His fingers ran across some type of hair. Had someone placed the rabbit inside as a joke? He nearly dropped the cauldron, but it didn't truly feel like rabbit fur. It was too soft. Closer inspection revealed that blood-matted blonde hair sat atop the cauldron. He parted some of the hair, which revealed two pale eyes staring at him.

He dropped the cauldron.

Krystal's head rolled out.